WITHDRAWN FROM LIBRARY

Fight Like a Man and Other Stories We Tell Our Children

FIGHT LIKE A MAN

& Other Stories We Tell Our Children

Christine Granados

UNIVERSITY OF NEW MEXICO PRESS • ALBUQUERQUE

© 2017 by Christine Granados
All rights reserved. Published 2017
Printed in the United States of America
22 21 20 19 18 17   1 2 3 4 5 6

Library of Congress Cataloging-in-Publication Data
Names: Granados, Christine, 1969– author.
Title: Fight like a man and other stories we tell our
children / Christine Granados.
Description: First edition. | Albuquerque :
University of New Mexico Press, 2017.
Identifiers: LCCN 2016017201 (print) |
LCCN 2016022902 (ebook) | ISBN 9780826357922
(paper : alk. paper) | ISBN 9780826357939 (electronic)
Classification: LCC PS3607.R3624 A6 2017 (print) |
LCC PS3607.R3624 (ebook) | DDC 813/.6—dc23
LC record available at https://lccn.loc.gov/2016017201

These stories originally appeared in the following
publications: *Huizache Magazine*: "She's Got Game";
*¡Arriba! Baseball: A Collection of Latino/a Baseball
Fiction*: "Good Father"; *Langdon Review of the Arts in
Texas*: "Shelf Life"; *NewBorder Anthology*: "stupids";
Pilgrimage: "Addressed"; *Callaloo*: "Haunts"; *Evergreen
Review*: "Fight Like a Man."

Cover photograph courtesy of Joel Salcido
Author photograph courtesy of Ken Esten Cooke
Designed by Lila Sanchez
Composed in Melior LT Std and ScalaSansOT

For Andy
Jose Andres Granados
1941–2014

Contents

FIGHT LIKE A MAN: A NOVELLA

CHAPTER ONE. **Curandera** 3

CHAPTER TWO. **Fight Like a Man** 7

CHAPTER THREE. **Haunts** 13

CHAPTER FOUR. **Just Us Girls** 23

CHAPTER FIVE. **Tension** 36

CHAPTER SIX. **The Seduction** 45

CHAPTER SEVEN. **Unraveled** 55

CHAPTER EIGHT. **La Ofrenda** 67

CHAPTER NINE. **Not What It Seems** 77

CHAPTER TEN. **Rest in Peace** 92

CHAPTER ELEVEN. **Bernie's Fortune** 99

SHORT STORIES

Shelf Life 115

A River of Misunderstanding 121

Addressed 129

stupids 134

Good Father 148

She's Got Game 157

Duck, Duck, Goosed 165

Acknowledgments 181

FIGHT LIKE A MAN

A Novella

CHAPTER ONE

Curandera

THESE PINK, YELLOW, and orange paint chips need to be swept off the sidewalk. I wonder who lets them pile up here. No wonder people call this place a dump. The adobe's been painted a hundred times. They have no pride. The chips stick to my heels. "Next," I hear. Without looking up, I step forward and bump the old woman in line in front of me.

"Excuse me." I raise my head and study the wild-haired, mossy señora, who does not look up but nods and continues staring at the cracks in the cement in front of her. I lean my back against the gray wall and look out at where the sand puddles against the curb across the street. To my right is the woman, and to my left is a young couple arguing. They have argued all morning long about any thing.

"Nah, man, Señora Jurado don't take insurance. Don't be stupid," the boy with cornrows says, running his hand over his hair.

"Well, how should I know? I've never been to a witch doctor," the young red-haired girl says.

"Curandera, Flor," he says.

"Yeah, that's what I said—witch doctor," she nods.

"No, man, that's the trouble with you. You don't listen. You got those big ears and they don't do you any good." He slaps the tips of her hair.

3

Neither is right, I think. Ana is a whore and a thief and I'm here to see her. So what does that make me? There was nowhere else I could go. How would I get three hundred dollars out of Sal without having to explain? Out of Regie? I touch my hair and push my sunglasses up on my nose. A dark man with one arm opens a screen door that has a thick fleece blanket with a picture of a lion where the wire screen should be. He yells from the adobe unit, "Next." Two more people before me and then I can get in and out and be rid of this thing once and for all. I hug my stomach tight.

"She can fix you up, Flor. Like that." The young boy snaps his fingers. "Witch doctor or whatever you think. I'm telling you, Señora Jurado is that good."

"I sure hope so," sighs the redhead, "because right now it looks like I have a cauliflower growing out my ass. It blocks my asshole so much that I have to pull my cheeks apart to fart."

"Too much information, babe, too much. I don't need to be picturing that." He laughs and walks away from her toward the street.

I cough to cover my laughter and the old woman looks up. "Granos are caused from too much sexo." She points a bony finger at the redhead.

"Excuse me? Jorge, what did she say?" She looks toward the street. "I didn't understand. What?"

Someone snorts like a pig and everyone in line starts to snort. The red-haired girl takes off down the sidewalk and I roll my eyes, stand upright, then walk across the street. The others in line scatter themselves in a slow, deliberate pace too. After the patrol car passes, I cross back over and stand in line where I was before. The old woman never moved.

"Soy adelante," she mumbles.

The one-armed man opens the screen door and before he can scream "next" the old woman is at his side. He shakes his head and pats her shoulder. A few minutes later the man has the woman by the collar and shoves her out the door. She doesn't resist, doesn't complain, just keeps repeating, "Que Dios te salve m'ija, te vas a ir al infierno."

4

"Next," he says, waving for me to come inside with the stub that used to be his arm.

When I walk through the screen door, I pause to take off my sunglasses. I hang them from the collar of my shirt as I step over two people lying on the cement floor on their stomachs with needles on the backs of their calves.

"¿Estás aqui por un mal?" he asks. "Are you sick?"

"Pienso que, que, que estoy em . . . em . . . pregnant." I say, staring at his arm, which ends mid-bicep. I want to know what happened to it, but before I think to ask him, he puts the nub under my face, lifts my chin, and studies my nose. He shakes his head then takes my left breast in his good hand and examines my face. When he sees me blink and suck air he says, "Sí, estás embarazada." He lets go of my breast.

He was so quick that I had no time to complain. I am unnerved from the roughness of the stump that he placed under my chin.

"Next," a deep, coarse, familiar voice calls out. "Eugenio, who's next?"

Eugenio points his stub to a pink door that is closed. Confused, I stare at the stub, then with his good arm he twists his hand like he is opening a knob and I understand.

"Adelante," the voice says.

I walk to the door and open it. The small room is painted teal and I stifle a nervous laugh. When I see the red, green, and white rebozo Ana Jurado wears over her black lace dress, I ball my fingers into a fist.

"¿Qué es el problema?" Ana says then looks up. She squints and lifts a small red lava lamp toward the doorway.

I sigh loud. "Yes, it's me. And I'm here for your tea."

Ana smiles, showing her brown gapped teeth, then places the lamp back on the cinder block next to the couch. "You pregnant?"

"Why else would I come?" My voice is low and firm.

"You still mad at me, Moní?" She pats the sofa for me to sit down. "You look just like your mother, all curves and hair. She kept her looks a long time, too."

5

I look down at Ana. "This isn't a reunion. Just gimme the tea y, ya, we'll call it even."

"You pay like everyone else." Ana strains to get up.

"That's not what I meant." I turn to walk out when Eugenio walks through the door with two Mason jars filled with what look like weeds.

"This is for killing the baby," Ana says, out of breath. She points to the green-tinted Mason jar and Eugenio hands it to me. I take it. "Cotton-root bark, vitamina y perejil. Drink it like a tea three times a day," Ana holds up three fingers, "for six days. The other is to help with the pain."

Eugenio waits for me to pull money out of my front pocket before handing me the clear glass jar, which I place under my armpit. I hold the green jar up toward the lamp with the cash between my fingers and watch Eugenio walk out.

I hear him yell "next" and Ana folds her hand over the twenty-dollar bill and my hand. "I didn't charge your father. No era así. I loved him too."

I wince and pull away from Ana's grip. The jar under my arm shatters on the cement floor. I hold the green jar tight. "Don't you dare talk to me about Vicente."

"Moní?" She looks at the glass on the floor before taking a step toward me. "You need more chicalote for the pain. Let me get Eugenio."

"Don't bother." I back out of the room. "You're a cheap substitute for a doctor and a wife. You live off of other people's pain."

"He loved your mother best," Ana yells as I pass the couple going by. I step on one of the women lying on the floor and stumble. I think I hear the woman hiss. Eugenio, light and quick, is next to me. He gives me his good arm, and I manage to keep my grip on the remaining jar, right myself, and walk out. Outside, the cutting sunlight makes me feel as normal as seeing snow capping the Franklins. I jump when the screen door slams shut behind me.

CHAPTER TWO

Fight Like a Man

SAL SITS HUNCHED over his plate, elbows on the table, fork in his right hand, spoon in his left. He reminds me of a brown bear trying to use silverware. I sit up when I hear the fork tines scrape ceramic. He is sick of tamales. I can tell by the way he puts down his fork and spoon, picks up the tamale, and lets it roll out of its skin, then plop. He eats with his fingers, bites into it, chews two times then swallows. He doesn't stop to sip his beer, to tell me about his day, or to look up. I'm glad because right now I am so mad I couldn't stand hearing a thing.

I keep seeing Regie's thin, dark body caked with sand. It should have been me that ended it this morning. I should have told him about my visit to the whore three days ago. He didn't kiss me, ask about the kids, play with my hair, or even help me with my shoes on the mesa at Red Sands. He seemed more jumpy than usual. I should have guessed. Should have known.

"We can't do this no more," he said, "because they're watching."

What I should have said was, "I don't care about any of that. You don't have to worry about me." But instead I said, "All right, it's too hot out here anyways. Take me home, yeah?" I have to tell him about this thing. I sip my special iced tea and try to remember if the whore told me to drink it for three days or six to get rid of the baby.

Sal clears his throat and points to his empty plate. "Everyone is going to like the tamales. You listening, Mónica?"

I focus on the pores that dot his nose. His face reminds me of a Ruby Red. I smile, thinking that if I touch it, it'll ooze.

He smiles back at me. "Don't worry. It's gonna be okay. They're going to like you. Are you going to eat that?" He scoops beans from my plate then licks them off the fork before I have a chance to answer.

"No, go ahead." I can't keep anything down, so I eat slow, hoping I won't have to throw up. He continues picking at my plate and I sigh. "Am *I* going to like *them*?"

"Of course—you love Bernie, no?" He licks his fork before digging it into my leftover lettuce. "Why wouldn't you like her mom and sister? You are all family."

I shoot Sal a dirty look and slide my plate away hard. It knocks over the Elvis saltshaker.

"If you don't want me to eat it just tell me." He drops his fork on his plate and it chips. He sighs and says, "Sorry. You've been in a bad mood since you been on that diet."

I look at the tea in my glass and wince. "I know."

"You don't need to drink that tea. You're fine to me." He touches my thigh.

I roll my eyes and turn to check the clock. It's nearly six, and the twins will be home any minute. Maybe they'll go to friends' houses and I'll get some time alone. "I can't even let a little weight creep up on me. I have to catch it early like a weed in the front yard. If you don't pick it, before you know it the front is covered and you won't want to do anything about it."

"Who told you you were fat?" Sal moves his plate away and places his forearms on the table. "Bernie? No, not Bernie. Someone at the store, while you shopped? Señora Provencio? A man?"

"No one. Believe it or not, I can decide for myself if I have to lose some weight." I grip my glass. It's already day three and I feel the same, probably because I can't keep the tea down. I don't think any of the tea is in my system because nothing stays in my stomach. It was the same with Gabe and Genny. I lost weight instead of gained. Well, everywhere but the belly. I have to stop rubbing my stomach. Those two purged and drained me. They're still doing it. What am I going to do with another one? They want so much from me. Things I don't have. Sometimes I wonder if they are the same being. All three of them, Sal especially, want, want, want, and what I want is to be alone. I get up to start the dishes, and I hear the door open. Halfway to the sink the door slams.

Startled, I drop the glass and it shatters on the tile floor. "Shit."

"Watch the door, goddamnit!" Sal's chair scrapes the floor, louder than the door. "Scare you?"

"Would you stop yelling already? It's not like we live in a mansion."

"Sorry, Dad." I hear Gabe, who is in the hallway.

Sal crushes the can in front of him and beer spills out the top. I shouldn't have mentioned the size of the house, but I want him to shut up. It's a great house. Our house is fine; it's just too close to the border, stirs up too many memories. Now there are no more Mexicans to hide. Mrs. Schmidt next door hates "wetbacks." She said if her husband were still alive he would shoot any Mexican that set foot near her house. Someday I'll tell her how many wetbacks we let stay in her backyard when she went on vacation to Alabama. I even let the women inside to use her restroom. I was young, angry, stupid when we bought this house. Back then I didn't want to be reminded of father's family in Juárez. Every Mexican I hid from the migra in the shed out back was a constant reminder that I wasn't part of Vicente Gomez's real family; that I didn't have a father; that I was alone. Sometimes it's easier to hurt Sal than tell him how I feel. I just need him to leave me alone.

As I pick up shards of glass, I think about Vicente and how nervous he'd get whenever a cop or the Border Patrol would drive by. I could always get him to smile by holding his hand. When I did, I imagined my being American could shield him. Those boulder-like teeth would poke through his thick lips; he would relax and not look so guilty.

Genny drops her books onto the counter and says, "Mom, it's not like Gabriel is bad. Actually, he's good. I mean compared to

9

other boys his age; they're getting arrested and stuff. Why are you wearing those again?"

"What the hell are you talking about? Get me the trash can." I point underneath the sink and have to slow down to catch my breath.

"Oh, hi, Dad," Genny says.

"Hey, flaca." Sal's mouth is full of something.

I don't want another girl. I couldn't stand the constant disapproval from two of them. "Start at the beginning."

Genny points to my pink jeans. "You've had them on for like three days."

"These are comfortable and I wash them every night. Besides, I look great in them." I look at my thighs. They seem larger than normal, and I look at Genny's slender legs. She's starting to fill out but won't ever have my chest. She has no idea how crazy she's going to make men. No idea. "Oh, never mind, just get me the can."

Genny stretches her long legs across the floor to avoid the glass and opens the cabinet under the sink. "Gabe got in trouble at school. He had to go to the principal's office and everything." She hands me the trash can. "I saw him when I was taking in the roll."

"Shut up. Nobody's getting arrested. Quit being so dramatic." Gabe walks into the kitchen, steps on the glass on the floor, and pushes his sister. I try not to smile, because there have been times I've wanted to shove Genny to shut her up too.

"Watch it, Gabe," I say. I mean he should watch where he is walking, but he takes it to mean he needs to leave his sister alone. He steps away from her. A boy would be easier to have, less judgment, less talking, less worry. I hear glass crunch. More mess. I can hear Sal sigh from the kitchen table, but I refuse to look at him. He's still mad about the house. I don't want to set him off, because then he'll take it out on Gabe. I don't have the energy to calm Sal *and* to explain to Gabe that his father's anger isn't his fault. I focus on picking up the big pieces as Gabe talks.

"Junior was getting all in my face. So I told him, 'Get out of my face, goddamnit!'"

I stand holding shards of glass in my hand. Relieved that I'm not dizzy, I look over at Sal and raise my eyebrow. His eyes narrow like they do when he's hurt. He shakes his head and walks into the other room. He's trying to punish me by leaving me alone, but I'm glad he is letting me handle this. Trying to comfort Sal when his feelings are hurt is like sweeping in the middle of a dust storm. I let out a long breath and wonder how to get this over with quickly so I can have time to myself. Maybe then the storm in the den will have blown over.

"Sorry, I didn't mean to cuss," Gabe says.

I try not to smile. Gabe must be in real trouble at school. He never apologizes. I wave the excuse away so Gabe will go on.

"Before I can even hit him, the teacher grabs me by my collar. Look, she almost ripped it off." He fingers the cotton collar. "And she says, 'You're going to the office right now, young man.' I didn't even hit him or nothing. I wouldn't have hit him. I don't think. Last thing I need is to mess up my hand and not be able to play the guitar."

I ball up my hands. I'm nauseated and light-headed. Gabe looks like his father when he's angry. Sal's dark, brooding eyes on someone so young almost make me smile. Gabe has grown so much since the start of the year—all lean and wiry. He is as tall as Regie. Regie is young enough to be my son. "Junior? You mean Junior Juárez? Is this Regie Junior? Who lives a block over?"

"Yeah, the one who's father is a marijuano."

"See, I told you he was in trouble, Mom." Genny slaps the counter top.

"Genny, go watch TV with your father. I have to talk to Gabe." I wonder what it would have been like if I had hit Regie with my fist this morning. "I know his father, Reginaldo. I know him very well. He goes by Regie too."

Genny lifts a foot in anger then looks down at the glass and decides not to stomp. "But I wanna stay. I'm the one that told you—"

"Alone." I point to the ceiling. "Go."

Genny takes a giant step across the floor again to avoid the glass. I'm thankful she's so considerate and am annoyed at Gabe's carelessness.

"Gabe? What the hell got into you?"

"Junior Juárez is just this big bully that everyone is afraid of and no one ever says nothing to him. He pushes everybody around and I knew some day he'd get to me." Gabe points to himself. "I've heard Dad. He said he comes from a family of losers."

I couldn't agree with Sal more. I should have hit Regie when I had the chance, and I should have known his son would be no good too. I have to get rid of his child. I will get rid of it. I nod my head and I close my hand around the shard of glass and punch the air. "Next time Regie Junior messes with you, you make sure and hit him. Hard. Hit him hard and fast so no one sees you. You hear me, m'ijo? Then tell him who you are. You're Gabriel Salvador Montoya."

Wide-eyed, Gabe stares at the blood from my hand dripping into the trash. "Ah, okay?"

I open my palm and drop the blood-stained glass into the garbage can and walk to the sink. Gabe doesn't move. "Do you hear me, Gabe? Tell him who you are—your full name. Understand? We never talked about this. ¿Oyes?"

"Yeah, Mom. I hear."

I look at the kitchen door for him to leave, and Gabe steps on the glass to get out. As I run water over the cut on my hand, I hear Genny's taunting. "You're in trouble. You're in trouble."

He yells, "Shut up," and she does.

CHAPTER THREE

Haunts

THERE IS NO way to look sexy carrying a fifty-quart pot of tama-les. If Bernie's not home and anyone sees me carrying this thing, I'm going to kill her. She said ten minutes; she'd be home in ten. I even gave her twenty to be safe, and I can see from here that her car's not in the driveway. I should have known better than to trust a Mexican to be on time. She's got five minutes. In five min-utes, I'm leaving everything on the steps—all of it, this olla, Sal, the kids, even Regie, and I'll let her deal with our father Vicente's funeral. She can figure out what to do with his ashes, and I'll go live in Juárez. Start another family like he did. Leave Bernie here in El Paso, since she loves it so much, thinks my life is so easy. She can deal with it all.

"Orale, Monica, what you got in the olla?" Elvira Provencio sits on the railing of her rock-and-cement patio I wish I could afford to have.

It would have to be this busybody, still in everybody's business. "Raw tamales, Señora Provencio. I can't stop because they're heavy."

"¿Estás loca? It's too hot to be outside. Why didn't you drive?" She rocks herself, trying to get enough momentum to stand.

"I know, huh? Crazy. It's that m'ijo's got the car for school. It's not so hot and I'm only a block away." The sweat from my fore-head sprinkles the cement because I'm walking too fast; I've got to keep moving before she gets up. If she's up, I'm stuck. "I'll see you."

I can see the door to Bernie's from here like a brown stain against the yellow stucco walls. Vicente brought the ridiculous thing to the house, when we lived there, from Chihuahua, said it was from Pancho Villa's mansion. Señora Provencio was outside then, too, when Vicente and his brother-in-law showed up in a sparkling-white van in the heat, in the middle of the day. The damn sun pushes everyone in the neighborhood inside, everyone except Señora Provencio. Not even a sandstorm can keep that metiche out of everyone's business. Thank God she shut up. I wait for Bernie on the stoop where the Señora can't see me. I feel ten years old again, here on the step, eyes closed, letting the sting on my butt settle and my jeans cool the hot cement.

Bernie still hasn't gotten rid of my mom's agaves. I can't believe Bernie bought the place or even wanted it. Mom's plants here in the front yard look like giant squids buried headfirst in the sand, their tentacles reaching toward the sun, ready to strike. Bernie told me she'd get rid of them when she moved in. If I were Bernie, I wouldn't want Vicente's other life slapping me in the face. She probably likes the pain of remembering her father was a cheat. Maybe even looks forward to the agave pricks. Agaves scare me like the sea movie. Just looking at them makes me all tense like when I watched the big underwater monster attack the submarine on TV as a kid. Sitting on the tile floor next to Vicente's chair would help calm me. I'd hold on to his arm; it seemed large enough to cover me back then, as it drooped over the armrest of the recliner when he slept. I would twist my fingers in that thick gold chain he wore on his wrist, wanting to wake him but knowing better, wondering if his kids on the other side did the same. The gleaming chain I played with danced orange in the blackness when I closed my eyes during the scariest parts of the movie. I wouldn't open them until its glow faded and my courage grew. The next morning I'd walk out into the front yard like Ned Land and try to kill all the squids. I tried every day, but only in the daytime. Pulled those thick, spiked leaves back toward me until they cracked. Once split, the blue-green tentacles rotted yellow then ash colored and finally rolled up like a carpet. Nothing stopped them from multiplying. Baby squids seemed to crawl out of their mother's bodies or up from the soft beige sand, stubborn and firm, unyielding like the sun. Constant like Vicente's weekly trips back to his other house. This isn't going to happen to Gabe and Genny. They're legitimate, and they'll never have to worry about their father. Sal comes home to us every night, and they don't have to worry that one day he might not show up. Mom would pack Vicente's suitcase every weekend, and I'd wait here in this spot like an idiot because they told me to, wondering if this was the last time I'd see him or if we'd lose him to his wife and kids. Mom didn't seem to worry, because she trusted that work would keep him coming back, but I wasn't so sure. No one is telling me to wait now, but still, I'm here. A middle-aged woman sitting on the same stoop getting stirred up by the same ghosts.

Here she comes. Damn Bernie. She's going to run her blue Road Runner into the house if she keeps opening the door before she puts the car in park. Waving like a fool, she looks just like Vicente when he brought home the door—Pancho Villa's door. I remember how he waved to Señora Provencio and then to me from the passenger side of the van. His side didn't shine; his side had the dull-gray-primer fender, but the rest of the van was spotless. That door and Mom's agaves are all I got left of that time, and I don't want either. I told Bernie to get rid of them when I sold her the house.

She's foolish and sentimental. And late, always late, and always in a hurry. She doesn't like waiting either. We both waited for Vicente in our separate worlds. God, she looks just like him with that wide-open smile. She's lucky she made it before I left.

"Ay, discúlpame. I'm sorry." Out of breath, she walks with a huff up the two steps, looks to either side, and lifts a small agave in a can near the door then takes a key from under it. "Why didn't you let yourself in?"

"Hurry up, this is heavy." Again, I wait as she unlocks the door. She has to push the heavy oak door with both hands. That smiling horned gargoyle that pokes out the farthest is worn gray from our touches. Inside, it's only a bit cooler than out. Stinky and Mancha poke their heads up from the black sofa with bored expressions and their tails wave in sync as if listening to some cat ranchera we can't hear.

"More tamales for the funeral next week?" Bernie pants and heads for the kitchen, ignoring the cats on the couch. "How long did you cook 'em?"

"An hour. It's not a funeral and it's in two weeks. You should remember, it's at your house." I follow behind, set the pot on the small, boxy stove. I grab a glass, fill it with water from the tap, then undo the top button of my pink jeans with one hand. I drink the glass of water in one gulp. "They're still not done."

Bernie looks at my belly. "Valgame, Dios. No. They should take thirty minutes. Pues, thirty-five at the most. We're paying our respects. It's a funeral. You're right, it's in two weeks."

The kitchen, long and narrow like a hall, is bookended by doorways, and Bernie's hip grazes my thigh as she passes me. She lets herself fall into a chair.

I set the lid in the stainless-steel sink, where it clashes like a cymbal. "We're dividing his ashes. It's just us, the family. What did I do wrong?"

"No se. Specially if you cooked them for an hour." Bernie's hands move in circles and Vicente's thick gold chain, which should be mine, trapped on her fleshy forearm, dings when she sets it down on the Formica. "We're going to need at least three hundred."

"You told me one hundred. Who else is coming?" I rub my belly, tug the zipper on my pants down, and sigh. "It doesn't matter. Lomart has hojas cheap right now on sale, three bags for two dollars. Regie told me."

Bernie stops smiling and her hazel eyes focus on my face before I realize my mistake.

"You still seeing him? I thought you were done?" she says.

"We are." I finger a tamale inside the pot and wish I were more careful with my words. "Sometimes. It's not serious."

"You look tired." Bernie places a hand on my arm. "Leading two lives takes a lot out of you. Tú mas que nadie should know."

I guess now is as good a time as any to tell her. "But anyway when we, I, drove over to Lomart to get the hojas and we, I, got out of the car, I rubbed my chichi on the door and I yelled in pain."

"You're driving around with him, in the day? You are crazy. Wait, your chichis hurt?"

I touch my breast and wince.

Bernie puts her hands over her mouth. "No? You can't be? Ay, Monica. Estás embarazada." She shakes her head.

I nod.

"Whose?" When Bernie puts her arm on the table, the gold chain tings. "Sit, sit."

I do what she says and whisper, "I haven't have had sex with Sal in . . . I dunno." I inch my zipper the rest of the way down.

"That explains a lot," Bernie says and points to my belly. "Your pants."

"These are the only jeans left that fit," I say. "Before I called you this morning, I wanted to eat the masa raw, as I mixed it, right then and there. Nobody was awake yet, Sal or the twins. Thank God because I ate four spoonfuls, asi, raw."

Bernie doesn't move. Stinky and Mancha purr and rub their sides on her legs. She gives a gentle kick and says, "What are you doing? Why? You're just like Vicen—"

"Don't say another word." I point my finger in her face. "I'm nothing like your father."

Bernie looks down at her cats and then places her other arm on the table in thought.

"Vicente never made tamales a day in his life." I smile.

"This isn't a joke, Monica. What are you going to do?" She picks up Mancha and scratches the white spot next to his ear. "Vicente told me that Josie craved raw tortillas when she was pregnant with you."

I stand, walk to the stove, and look in the pot. "What I don't get . . ." I wipe my eyes. "They're still all chewy. Soft, like baby food. I thought you might know what I did."

17

I flinch when the chrome legs of the chair tilt as Bernie sighs and leans toward the stove to get a look inside the pot. To avoid looking at the legs and thinking at all, I pick up the stiff dishcloth in the sink, run water over the rag, ring it out, and wipe down the windowsill. Try to clean the sandy grit that films everything in this place.

"Una hora cooking on your stove." Bernie's thick brows crease and Mancha jumps out of her lap.

I clean off the pink radio that has been sitting on the sill since I lived in the house and I click it on. I close my eyes and sway to Jose Alfredo's " . . . y mi palabra es la ley . . ."

"Ay dios, why are you listening to that?" Bernie rolls her eyes and stomps her foot. The cats scatter.

"What? Because you live on this side now, you can't listen to Mexican music anymore?"

"I'll always be Mexicana pero ya vivo aquí." Bernie stands, lets out a breath, spits on her hands, and looks into the pot.

The sound of Bernie spitting reminds me of my mother. Josie had hissed and spat as Vicente and Bernie's uncle had worked on hanging the front door with its gargoyles. Only back then I didn't know it was Bernie's uncle at the house; I didn't know about Bernie. Mom didn't stop until Vicente left the claw hammer hanging in the trim and pushed her back into the house. He had screamed that the door was a part of him, who he was, straight from Pancho Villa's house. She had yelled back that she didn't need to be haunted by the ghost of another country, and that one womanizer in her house was enough for her to deal with. Back then, I thought it was the door she was mad at and thought nothing of the man Vicente had brought with him.

Bernie says, "I would have helped you make them."

"No, I don't want any help. I like being alone." I toss the towel in the sink and it lands with a dull thud on the lid. Bernie looks hurt and is probably disgusted at how American that sounded. "It's that it was nice alone in the kitchen and my hands were busy and I bought this brand-new olla. I wanted to be the first to use it."

18

Bernie sits back down and nods toward the pot. "¿Qué les pasó?"

"Well, I put the water in and put the hojas on the bottom nice and thick like Mom. I mean Josie."

"You can call her Mom," Bernie chuckles. "She's gone."

I shake my head. "She'd kill me if she heard me call her that." I run my finger across my throat. "Before I know it, it's already seven o'clock and I've got twelve dozen made and ready to go. So I put them on the stove to cook, start cleaning up, and go wake the kids for school." I take long deep breaths, trying to stop the tears that are coming. "Jesus, I'm pregnant. I'm fucking pregnant. You believe it? I thought I couldn't get pregnant. My tilted uterus wasn't tilted far enough."

Bernie claps and huffs to stand. "That explains everything."

"No, Bernie, you can't get pregnant making tamales." I open a drawer near the stove. "Why didn't you just leave everything where it was? I can't find anything in Josie's kitchen anymore."

"Cállate. This is my house now." She looks into the pot. "When you're cooking tamales, the cook can't leave the kitchen or they'll come out como pintos."

"What? What are you talking about? I never left the house." I open two other drawers before I find two oven mitts.

"Yes, but you left the kitchen and they won't cook." Bernie smiles and shows her teeth, which are white and crowded together.

"That's crazy." I wave the Santa Claus and Mrs. Claus mitts in the air and sigh the way Vicente did when he came back after yelling at Josie about the door. Half his face was red; he had smiled with a shrug and a look that was half apology and half "she's loca." I loved his smile, the way his teeth were packed tight in a small space like the rocks at Hueco Tanks. Bernie has teeth like his, and just like Vicente they don't go with her flat face, as if they don't belong in her mouth, but they make me feel good when I see them.

Bernie closes her mouth. "I've been cooking tamales for ten years ya, and I left the kitchen plenty of times, and every time I do, they don't cook. They don't come out. Te estoy diciendo; you can't leave. Aunque sea un pie, a single foot."

"I don't know, Bernie." I slide the oven mitts on and lift the large silver pot off the stove. I drain the water into the sink and dump the masa-filled cornhusks in too.

"Why do you use those?" Bernie uses her fake nails like tongs to lift a tamale.

I look at the mitts on my hands and laugh. "Habit." I study the inside of the pot. With the mitts still on, one by one, I lift the cornhusks that line the bottom. They are as thin as the prefab door Vicente had taken away from the house. Its replacement was made in Spain. Vicente had said it made him feel like a king. A king without a crown, he would sing in Spanish. A king, like the crazy English one, who switched women as the mood or situation suited him. I frown.

"No, you should never leave the kitchen. Te digo." Bernie unwraps the tamale and tastes it. "Needs salt."

When I get to the bottom of the pot I fish out a steel rack. "How stupid."

"¿Quién?"

"Me. Look." I shove the steamer bottom near Bernie, who leans back. "I was cooking these tamales like my mom. And she used the hojas for the steamer."

"Steamer?"

"This, this." I hold up the silver circle. "My mom didn't have these newfangled pots with steamers built in. How stupid. I should have known."

"Fangled? ¿Qué? What are you talking about?" Bernie makes a face when she puts another piece of mushy tamale in her mouth, but she chews it anyway.

"Mom used the hojas as a steamer." I lift the round steel rack toward Bernie again. "I don't need the hojas. When I put them on top of this it covered the holes, made it impossible for the tamales to cook."

"Ah, tapadas. I get it. Maybe that's what you should have done when you were with Regie."

I don't laugh. It's not funny. Instead I drop the steel rack on the stove and throw the mitts at Bernie then march out of the kitchen toward Vicente's recliner. As I sit, I'm pricked in the bicep by an agave on an end table. I take its leaf in my hands and bend it. Smile when I hear the soft pop. I killed so many of the hard leaves on the sly when I was little that my mother thought the dirt in our yard was cursed, so she brought them all inside. Her tequila farm Vicente used to call it. Why Bernie kept them all, I don't understand.

"¿Qué dije? You're so emotional." Bernie heads toward me. "You leave my plantas alone."

"They're not yours." I pop another miniature leaf.

"They are mine. I bought this house with my own money and I like it exactly the way it is."

"You're sick is what you are. You want to live in a museum to your dad's other life." I point to the ceiling.

"At least I'm not pregnant, making another bastard child." She sits on the couch.

I put my face on the armrest, which is a darker brown than the rest of the chair, and I cry.

Bernie sighs and we listen to Juan Gabriel sing "Amor Eterno." After a few minutes she says, "I'm sorry. I didn't mean it. I think, I think you need to go see Señora Jurado."

I look up at her. "I did."

"Are you joking me?" Bernie waves her hands in the air. "You told me Ana was just a whore."

I hear the kitchen radio's "tan tan" that ends every song. "She is. You don't know her like I do. I'm not stupid."

"She helped my sister when she was pregnant." Bernie is quiet and the trill of the radio announcer breaks the silence in the house.

I lift my index finger and then rub it against my thumb. "She's just a puta. No looks, no body, but a good memory. She remembers how to seduce people. She's been doing it all her life. It comes natural. She has that one gift. She can still get the last penny out of a man's pocket."

Bernie pulls the gold chain loose from her forearm and rubs the indentation it made on her flesh. "Graciela was still able to have kids after she got rid of the first one."

"Yes, Ana knows her herbs. Still, she mixes them with castor oil because she knows, she knows Mexicans are dumb. She knows they won't believe anything that can help them can taste good." I shut my eyes at my mistake, then add, "I don't mean to bad mouth—"

"You're not saying nothing I haven't." Bernie touches the bracelet. "I deserved that."

I eye the chain on her wrist. "Graciela was pregnant in school?" I stand. Rub my stomach.

"Her breasts were tender like yours and she knew. She knew she couldn't have no baby and go to school, so we went. She drank the hierbas and on the sixth day she went to the bathroom and . . ." Bernie presses her hands to her chest. "Well, she helped Graciela."

"The herbs helped Graciela." I trace the crack in the linoleum floor with the heel of my pump.

"Not a day goes by que no piensa en su bebé." She taps her forehead.

"Well, I don't want any more. And the witch was the last person I wanted to go to with this." I point to my stomach. "Sal might like another one, but what if this one doesn't look like him? I gotta go drink my tea."

CHAPTER FOUR

Just Us Girls

WHEN GENNY CUTS the car engine, I hold up the white paper bowl in my hand. "Take a bigger bite, will you?"

She rolls her eyes before she bites into the churro, as I empty my purse to make room for a foot-long chili dog sitting on the dash of the car.

"It's still too long?" I pick up the bowl and hand it to her.

Genny says something, but bits of deep-fried dough sprinkled with cinnamon and sugar fall out of her mouth.

"What? Don't talk with your mouth full, grosera. Here." I hand her my wallet, and she takes it with her free hand, then I layer the bottom of my purse with napkins from my lap. "You're going to have to pay because I have all the food."

Genny takes a bite of the churro, chews, and swallows. "Is Bernie coming or not?"

"What?" I place the chili dog into my purse. "Don't talk with your mouth full."

With a sigh, Genny hands me the dessert, which I put in my purse, and pulls on the black plastic handle to unlock her door. She puts one long, thin leg out of the car and gets out of the passenger side. As she walks behind the car and opens the door for me, I see her watching a tall, young man. He takes my breath away too. In fact, I can't take my eyes off of him. An elderly woman clutches his muscled bicep and he keeps a slow pace

23

without a hint of frustration. He holds a free hand out in front of him to stop a car in the parking lot from pulling out. The way he holds his arm in the air is identical to my father. I can't stop watching him. Could this be another one, like me? He looks about the right age. They make their way toward the building, slow and deliberate. His sleeveless shirt is wet at the small of his back. I step out of the car, legs closed, the way I taught Genny to get out, and she holds out a hand for me to grab.

"Careful," I say, "or the chili will spill all over my bag. And yes, Bernie's bringing drinks."

"Why'd you have to bring this one?" Genny pats my green patent leather bag as if it were a puppy. "I mean, a chili dog in an expensive bag like this? Since when do you even eat chili dogs, Mom? The only people I know who eat this stuff are pregnant. Katie Daniels said it was the only thing she could keep down before she had her little boy."

"How is she doing? She still in school?" I touch my stomach.

"No, no, she works at the hot-dog stand in the mall," Genny smiles. "I know, I know, funny, right?" She pats my shoulder.

"Don't do that." I stand next to the car waiting for the sting to go away.

"Sorry. I forget. Why are you always sunburned? You need to stop laying out." Genny hangs on the door and looks toward the guy we noticed before.

"I'm not always. I look better tan." I slam the car door shut because I'm embarrassed about lying to Genny. I can't keep my eyes off the young man standing in the ticket line. "Here, you hold it. It hurts too much. You can use it. Who are we checking out?"

"Checking out? What? Mom, you need to go back to work or something." Genny steps over gum in the parking lot, then giggles.

"Why, because I notice good-looking men?" I stop walking. I worry that she knows about me and Regie.

"So you won't be wrinkled when you're old." Genny takes my elbow. I humor her and don't pull away. "It just seems like you're always sunburned."

24

"My job is to look good." I can't help but laugh. She is so young. I can't remember ever being so young. "Speaking of looking good, the Mexicano in the tee was very handsome, no?"

"I don't know what you're talking about." Genny picks up the pace.

"You know." I nod my head and let her lead me toward the line for the movie. "The guy could be family."

"God, Mom, you're already marrying me off." She gives my arm a squeeze.

I let her think that's what I meant. We both step up the curb and head toward the ticket-booth line. The young man looks behind him, first at me, and then at Genny. I think I'm going to like him. The elderly woman tugs at his T-shirt and he turns to her. "I don't want to see anyone half-naked or no one dying."

"Well then we should go home now, Abuela." The young man laughs.

Genny is standing directly behind him and I have to do something or else Bernie will never believe me. I take an extra-wide step as I turn to look for Bernie in the parking lot and Genny falls against the man.

"I'm so sorry," Genny says, then glares at me.

"You really shouldn't drink so much, m'ija." I wink at her.

"Mom! Stop it." She takes the bag off her shoulder.

"Don't worry about it." He turns and grins.

"I've got a bottle here in my bolsa." The elderly woman pats her bag and smiles.

I tip my head back and raise my thumb toward my mouth and everyone laughs, except Genny.

"Really sorry." Genny, nervous, dusts off his shoulders, and when she realizes she is touching him her eyebrows arch.

"You should take your grandmother to watch the movie we're going to see." I avoid Genny's glare. "It's a love story with no guns and no nude scenes."

"Yeah, I was wondering what to watch." He points over his shoulder. "She doesn't like all the violence, but I don't want to be bored."

"I know what you mean." I touch Genny's arm and she moves away. "Genny here didn't want to come because the movie was too boring for her."

"No, it's—"

I place my hand on her arm and grip it so she can't move away. I scan the man's lips, nose, eyes, and hairline, looking for a family resemblance. "She's just trying to be nice. She wanted to see the robot movie."

"No—" Genny says.

"Well, I don't," the grandmother says. "I'd rather watch what you're seeing."

I wink at the woman, and she winks back. "Why don't you come with me, and Genny and your grandson can go see the movie they like."

Genny and the young man look at each other, and she stares at her feet. He sways on his heels, then looks at his grandmother. A lock of hair falls from his side part onto his forehead, and he combs it back with his fingers. Vicente used to do the same with his blue-black hair.

The woman is all smiles. She waves. "Sí, sí vayan. I'm okay here with . . ."

"Monica, I'm Monica Montoya." I hold my hand out.

"Mucho gusto." The woman takes it and gives it a squeeze. "I'm Adela Diaz and this is my grandson, Danny."

"Nice to meet you both." I shake Danny's hand. "This is my daughter, Genoveva."

"Genny. Genny, just call me Genny," Genny says as she reaches for Danny's hand.

"Do you like churros, Señora Diaz?" I give her an arm to hold on to.

I hear Danny. "How about it?"

"Uh, okay," Genny says.

Señora Diaz and I walk toward the theater entrance. "We can wait inside with the air conditioning while these two get our tickets."

The hum of arcade games, the smell of stale popcorn, and the rush of cool air give me goose bumps.

"Well, that was nice of you." Señora Diaz holds my arm as we walk like a bride and groom toward an overweight usher sitting on a barstool. "You're very generous with my grandson Danny."

"He looks like a nice boy, and Genny is a good kid." I readjust the strap of my purse on my shoulder.

She laughs. "Yes, I knew right away."

"She's pretty slow, right?" I smile.

"She'll learn."

I see that Danny holds the door open for Genny, and they both wave the tickets in the air. I wave back. Genny's light skin is flushed and her dark hair bounces. The girl has no idea how crazy she's going to make someone someday.

Danny seems taller than before as he hands his grandmother her ticket.

Genny gives me two tickets and keeps my wallet.

Before I give the usher my tickets, I step close enough to him that his soapy scent is strong, and I place my chest in his view. "You think I could leave a ticket here for my sister?"

"Well, we're not supposed to. You really should . . ." He can't keep his eyes off my cleavage. I inhale to give him a better view as he points toward the ticket booth.

I touch his arm. "She's just parking the car, and I've got to get Mother here seated. She can't stand for long."

"Yeah, of course. What she look like?" he says to my chest.

"She's big and beautiful. You won't miss her. She'll be running toward you and her shirt will probably be unbuttoned, or her pants, or her shoelaces untied. Her name's Bernadette Gomez. She'll tell you."

I hand him my ticket and lick my lips. His eyes still locked on my breasts, he scans the tickets in my hand. He points to his right. My hip brushes his crotch and his face flushes. Not bad, I think, and I laugh as Señora Diaz and I walk by. Genny and Danny pair up and hand him their tickets, and he points to the left.

27

"We'll meet right out here after the movie," I yell as Señora Diaz and I walk into a line that is twenty people long.

Genny yells "okay" and walks on, while Danny gives us a double thumbs-up behind her back and we both laugh. I might have made a mistake about him. He may not be related at all. Genny seems excited.

"I'm not so sure about Genny," I whisper as we move into the dark theater blasting movie previews. I hope she'll be able to handle herself. I'm comforted knowing we're in a public place and she'll be safe.

Señora Diaz touches the carpeted walls and slows down, waiting for her eyes to adjust. Several people pass.

I let go of her arm. "I see three seats. Lemme get them before someone else does."

"Go, go," she says.

I march three steps up the aisle. "Excuse me," I say. A family of four shifts their legs to let me pass. Seven seats down the row toward the center of the theater I stand and wait.

The father and mother of the family hold Señora Diaz's arm as she walks toward me. She sits in the first available seat and sets her purse on the seat between us. As I settle in she leans across the seat and says, "What about that churro you were talking about?"

"I've also got a chili dog we can split." I place my purse next to Señora Diaz's.

The old woman laughs and cups a hand around her mouth and says, "I've got some french fries here in my purse but we don't got nothing to drink."

"Don't worry about that. My sister is coming and she said she's bringing the drinks."

"Ah, qué suave. I'm set then." She shifts her weight in the seat.

"You think the kids got food?" I take out the churro from my purse on the seat.

Señora Diaz takes it. She nods. "Oh yes, Danny probably went to get them both something. He has a good job at the refinery."

"Oh, yeah, that is a good one. My husband works there. He's been there for fifteen years. He might know Danny."

28

"Oh, m'ijo doesn't work at the refinery here. It's in . . . in . . . I can't remember the name of the city." Señora Diaz shifts in her seat.

"Does he have his own place?" I change the subject for her.

She places the dessert on her lap. "No, no, m'ijo lives with me. His mother left when he was in diapers."

I ease the chili dog out. My mouth waters and I imagine the baby kicks. "And you've been taking care of him. How wonderful."

She digs into her purse. "He's a good boy, easy."

"Aren't they all?" I hold the flap up for her. "What about his father?"

"I dunno." She sets the fast-food fries in the armrest cup holder.

"It must be hard." I look at the screen previews and hope Genny finds Danny as interesting as I'm finding him.

We set our food on our laps and watch the screen. Before long, I hear the familiar husky voice, "¿Donde están? Ay, I can't see a damn thing in here." People giggle and I stand and wave with my dog in hand. "Ah, hay están."

The family of four stands and allows Bernie, who is holding a black tote twice the size of mine, to pass. Bernie gives me a hug and kiss.

"Sit down, sit down." Señora Diaz lifts her bag off the seat and sets it on the floor.

"This is Señora Diaz, Bernie," I say.

Bernie turns to face her and gives her her right hand. "Ah, mucho gusto, good to meet you. ¿Y Genny?" She looks over at me.

Señora Diaz squeezes Bernie's hand. "She's watching a movie with my grandson."

Bernie laughs and looks over at me. "What did you do?"

All three of us laugh and someone from behind whispers, "Shhh. Sit down."

I take my purse from the middle seat and touch the sticky floor with my toes, as if testing bath water. I look to the left of my seat and to the right and set my purse on the floor in front of me. "Yes, yes, sit."

The woman sitting next to me stands. "Oh, no, not on the floor. We'll move down one so you can put your purse on the seat and hold on to your money."

"Thank you." I try to think up a good deed to pass on to someone else.

Bernie sits down and places the tote on her lap. She reaches into it, pulls out a drink the size of a half-gallon jug of milk, and hands it to Señora Diaz. "For you, señora."

"This will last me ten minutes." Señora Diaz takes it like she's been waiting for it.

"Oh, you picked up a comedian, Mónica," Bernie whispers as she hands me a drink of equal size.

"Thanks," I whisper.

"Hold this, m'ija." Bernie hands Señora Diaz a large Styrofoam cup with a lid.

Señora Diaz takes the cup while looking at the screen. When she looks down at the cup, she whispers loud enough for me to hear, "You brought menudo?"

"Es que, I was just sitting down to eat when Mónica called." Bernie points at me.

"Menudo, Bernie? Menudo?" I laugh. "And you didn't even bring bolillos?"

"I did. Los tengo aquí." She feels around in her purse some more and pulls out a roll.

Giggles from people sitting behind and in front of us fill the theater.

Bernie continues digging in her bag. "Aha," she says and taps the spoon on Señora Diaz's arm.

"¿Quieres french fries?" asks Señora Diaz.

We giggle and are shushed by the people in front of us.

"M'ijo is a very good boy. He vacuums my bedroom, but I still wash his clothes." Señora Diaz fidgets, trying to get comfortable in a flimsy wrought-iron chair near the video arcade.

Bernie and I roll our eyes at each other.

Genny is walking ahead of Danny, who is talking and trying to catch up.

Bernie gasps. "Ah, he looks like—"

"I know." I put a finger across my lip, then nod toward Señora Diaz.

Bernie frowns. "Except for the teeth."

When they reach us, Genny gives Bernie a quick hug and kiss and whispers something in her ear.

"Did you like the movie?" Bernie looks Danny up and down.

"Yes, we loved it. It was great." He holds a hand out. "You must be Genny's aunt."

"Yes, yes." She takes his hand in both of hers and squeezes gently.

"It was okay." Genny looks right at me. "Well, it was great meeting you. Thanks for everything."

Bernie lets Danny go and puts an arm out for Señora Diaz to take. "Thanks for the fries, señora."

"Next time I'm bringing menudo." Señora Diaz takes Danny's arm.

"Abuela, you can't bring menudo to a movie," Danny laughs.

"Oh, you can. It was good, too, m'ijo." She pats his arm.

"Really? They sell it here?" Danny points toward the concession stand.

"No, but they should," Señora Diaz says.

Genny is pulling at my hand and Danny says, "You'll have to tell me all about it on the way home. Hey, Genny, can I get your number?"

Genny frowns at me and then turns to Danny. "Sure. Lemme write it down for you."

I take a pencil out of my near-empty purse and hand it to her. She scribbles a number on the back of her ticket stub and writes Genny Gomez on it. I don't say a word.

"I hope to see you soon, m'ija." Señora Diaz gives Genny a hug.

"Yeah, me too." Danny moves to hug her but Genny sticks out her hand for him to shake.

"It was great meeting you both." She fake smiles and pats Danny on the back.

As I hug Señora Diaz, Bernie and Genny walk toward the exit.

"Don't forget Chihuahuita. I live in apartment ten. Everyone knows us—just ask whoever you see when you come."

"I know right where that is. I'll stop by when I go to the perfumería. I go almost every month." I look toward the exit. "I gotta go now, me van a dejar."

I hug Señora Diaz one more time, and then Danny. He squeezes me a little too hard and holds me a little too long. I race to catch up to Genny and Bernie.

"Wait up," I yell, but only Bernie stops.

Genny pushes the glass door open and walks out. Bernie and I walk through it into the blinding sunshine.

Genny is waiting for us inside the car. As we get inside, she revs the engine.

"He was that bad, huh?" I laugh.

Genny looks straight ahead. "Worse. I wish you would stop doing that. Tía, where's your car?"

"Just take me to your house. We'll come and get it later. I want to hear."

"How bad could it have been?" I start to put my things back in my purse.

"He talked through the entire movie." Genny won't look at me.

"That's good, no?" Bernie's face is poking between the front seats.

"About himself," she says. "He wants me to come to his house on the West Side. It has twenty rooms and thirteen bathrooms."

"Really?" I look up from my purse.

"His grandmother didn't say anything about twenty rooms," Bernie says. "They live together in Chihuahuita."

"Then he was such an idiot that he couldn't remember how many rooms he told me his house had, and with each new story about polo matches and jet plane rides the number of rooms in the house increased."

"Sounds awful." Bernie slaps my shoulder.

"Ay, don't," I say.

"You sunburned *again*?" Bernie pinches my shoulder.

I suck in air until the sting stops.

"What's wrong with you?" Bernie says. I move forward before she can pinch me again.

Genny laughs out loud as she puts the car in reverse. "You deserve it."

"I'm sorry, Genny."

"He was awful," she said.

I place my hand on Genny's arm, which is on the steering wheel. "When he hugged me good-bye he gave me one of those hard, long hugs like he was feeling me up."

"No wonder he's out on the weekend with his grandmother." Genny's thick hair bounces as she shakes her head.

"You gave him your number?" Bernie's voice is too loud.

"No, she didn't," I caress Genny's arm.

"How'd you know that?" Genny looks at me for the first time since we got in the car, and I'm relieved that she's forgiven me.

"I saw you write Genny Gomez on the paper. Good one."

"Don't ever do that to me again. Ever." Genny pulls out of the parking space.

"How else are you going to meet boys?"

"He wasn't even a boy. He was in his twenties." She stops for a family walking toward the theater.

"There's nothing wrong with older men." I keep my eye on the thin man holding a toddler in his arms and walking ahead of the woman. I smooth the fabric over my stomach.

"She's sixteen, Mónica." Bernie rubs her knuckles against my arm.

"He looked like a nice kid." The woman pushing an empty stroller looks at me. I look away.

"He looked like Vicente," Bernie says.

"Acted like him, too, apparently." Genny drives on.

"I wanted Bernie to see him. I couldn't believe the resemblance," I say.

"So you sacrificed me?" Genny hits the steering wheel.

33

"I didn't hear many complaints." I smile. "You seemed more than happy to go with him."

"Well, he was handsome, but when he opened his mouth, geesh," Genny says.

"My father was the opposite," Bernie says. "He was ugly to look at, but once he opened his mouth and started talking he was handsome."

I nod. "Yeah, that's how he seduced all his women."

"Women?" Bernie touches my back. "Vicente had no others."

"Do you believe that?" I turn to look at her.

"Only Josie and my mother."

"You're joking me, right? Bernie?" I reach for her but she sits back and I miss. "Did he tell you that?"

The hum on the wheels on the road fills the silence.

"He did." I point to Bernie. "And you believed him?"

Bernie kicks my seat so hard I jump. "Speaking of family, you know my sister and mom want to bring something to the funeral? What can they bring? Can you believe they don't want to stay in my house?"

Genny peeks over at me and I point to the road and say, "You're going to get us killed. Watch where you're going." Then to Bernie I say, "It's not a funeral. I'm not surprised they don't want to stay the house. It's weir—"

"Why haven't I ever met them?" Genny says.

"I haven't either," I say.

Bernie laughs. "You both are. Everyone is. I wanted to ask a favor."

I turn to look forward, away from Bernie's smile. I know I am not going to like what she is about to ask. "Let's hear it."

"Can we have Vicente's funeral, I mean, ash ceremony, at your house? Es qué mine is too little." Bernie is working her fingers in and out of the gold chain on her wrist.

"Yes, of course." Genny claps a hand on the steering wheel.

"Wait a minute." I touch Genny's arm again and squint at Bernie. "I thought this was going to be a small ceremony with just family. I hear you're inviting our neighbors."

Bernie fans her face with her hands. "It wasn't me. It's my sister, my mom, and my tío. I . . . I think they are nervous to meet you. Plus, they don't like the idea of being in her, the, your old house."

"*They're* nervous?" I turn around and look out my window. What if she doesn't like me, sees too much of my mother in me, and they're at my house? What if we argue?

"I'll help you." Genny reaches for my hand with the other on the wheel. "We can finally meet everyone and you and Bernie can figure out what to do with Vicente's ashes."

I take it and squeeze.

"Come on, Mom, I know his ashes have been bugging you." She squeezes back, then lets go of me to make a turn.

"I don't know. I don't think I'm ready for this at my house." I put a fingernail in my mouth and quickly take it out, remembering Josie's scoldings.

"What's to be ready? Te ayudo." Bernie's face is between the seats again.

"And I'll help too." Genny puts the car in park. "I want to meet your other sister."

"She's not my sister." I touch the door handle.

"Well, still I want to meet Bernie's sister." Genny takes the key out of the ignition.

I pull the door handle. "Yes, yes, so do I."

Bernie claps.

"There's still the ashes to talk about, too." I step out of the car.

Bernie opens her car door and looks up at me. "I don't think mami cares what we do with the ashes."

"Oh, you'd be surprised what people care about when it comes time to do something."

CHAPTER FIVE

Tension

I HAVE TO get my mind off Regie, the ashes, and the party. I wish I would have thought to get my wallet from Genny before she left with Bernie. Sal's wallet is still in his pants, since he got home after I did. I could be at Rocky's already if I had money instead of stuck in Gabe's closet like a ladrona looking for cash to take. Where is it? Where'd Gabe put the box? Score. He's smart to put it high on the shelf. All ballerina, I'm barely tall enough to get it. He's home. Shit.

"We're going to my room," he yells from the living room.

"Who's your friend?" Sal yells back.

"It's Darlene. We're gonna do some homework," Gabe says.

"¡Eh!" Salvador yells.

"Hi, Mr. Montoya," she yells back.

These cheap bifolds never close all the way. If I duck under his hanging clothes, he may not see me or look directly at the crack between the doors. I wonder where I dropped the lid to the shoebox? I cover my mouth until I'm calm. Already Gabe is strumming that guitar. I lean forward to look out. I can see Gabe's serious face, and he is chewing his fat lower lip as he strums the strings. The girl with him has light-brown hair that covers most of the red letters on the back of her white T-shirt.

"Keep it quiet!" Salvador yells, and I squeeze the roll of quarters in the box.

Gabe gets up and kicks the sticker-filled bedroom door shut just like his father. I can see both him and the girl sitting on the bed. They are facing me. She is touching Gabe's hand. I can't move. I don't want to be here. I don't want to see this. Gabe looks like his father. His teeth are so white they look like glitter rocks. I feel inside the box as I stare at Gabe, who keeps grinning. He never smiles this much. I stroke Gabe's baby shoes—crocheted by his abuela. Sal's mother dotes on Gabe. Still, these were the only shoes that stayed on his big feet when he was a baby. Jesus, I can't have another one. I don't want to go through it all over again. How could I have been so stupid? Another baby and a funeral? I need to get out. Underneath the booties I find a wad. There are fives, tens, probably seventy dollars here. I peer out. The bills fall as the girl kisses Gabe's ear as he strums his guitar.

"I don't think we should be in here with the door shut," she says in a whisper.

"If we're quiet, Darlene, he won't mind." Gabe tilts his head toward the door as he strums.

"Where's your mom?" she says.

Darlene? Who is this Darlene? Was she there when Gabe was fighting with Regie Junior? I think of Regie and I want to leave. Get out of this house. I open and close my eyes. I see the navy-blue walls in Gabe's room and the navy-blue elephant lamp that sits on three cinderblocks he painted black.

"I dunno, probably shopping or something. She's not around much." He brings his ear down toward the strings to hear the chords he plays.

"I like the guitar, too." She leans into Gabe's left arm. "A friend of mine told me that it's all about tension."

Gabe looks up at her for the first time since they entered the room. "What do you mean?"

"Well, you get this beautiful sound from these two points of tension." Darlene takes one hand and places it on Gabe's shoulder and uses the other to touch his hand on the fret board.

I bite my hand to muffle my laughter. The silent giggles die when I see Gabe lean over and kiss Darlene, and then he runs his hand to her breast.

Here we go. I feel like Genny rolling my eyes. What is it that their mothers teach them? I shake my head and watch Gabe ease the guitar out from between their bodies and set it gently on the floor. I'm thankful that he is so careful with the hundred-dollar instrument. Darlene lies on his bed like it is hers. I can only see their hips; I snatch glimpses of Gabe's hand rubbing her upper body. Darlene moans.

"Stop, Gabe. Your dad will hear us."

I look away but hear moist smacks, heavy breathing and giggles, and then, worse, quiet.

When I peek again, Gabe is digging his fingers into her crotch like he's pulling the small weeds that grow between the gravel in the front yard.

"Ouch! You're hurting me," she says.

I roll my eyes. He may be my son but he's also half Sal's.

"Sorry. I'm sorry. How's this?" Gabe keeps his fingers straight and caresses her pubic bone.

I have to get out of here.

"Better," she says. "I'd like it even more if we were somewhere else."

Gabe lifts her T-shirt. He kisses her stomach as he helps her slip off the T-shirt.

I straighten my back and I wonder if I should make noise, interrupt. We don't need another pregnancy. We can't afford another one. I shouldn't be here. I think of Regie and our rushed times together. Maybe it's always the same. No, sex with Sal is slow, drawn out, and sometimes clumsy and silly. The pleasure he gives is accidental, but when it does happen it's worth it. It lasts . . . It's too quiet. I lean in to get a better view, and this girl has no shame, no shame at all.

"Stop, Gabe. We'll get caught." Gabe fumbles with her bra.

"If you're quiet. Shhh." He talks to her breasts and undoes her jean shorts, then she slips them off herself like panties, which she does not wear. "And stop laughing so much."

"I'm scared. I want to stop."

"Me too," he stands and undoes his pants. They fall to his ankles, followed by his white briefs, then he inches between her legs.

"You don't look it," she whispers.

I bite my finger, inhale deep, and look down at Gabe's shoes. The bills fell inside his tennies.

"Ouch. No. Not there," she raises her voice.

I couldn't tell if Gabe was using protection. Sal needs to talk to Gabe about women, but I'll probably have to do it myself.

"Did you hear that?" Darlene says. "Stop. I heard something."

"Shhh, shhh," Gabe says.

When I cup my hand to my mouth, the bills I picked up smell like smoke.

"Help me," he says, breathless. "Can't you see?"

"No. Stop," she says.

I hide my face in both hands. I remind myself to look for Gabe's cigarettes later.

"What's wrong now?" Gabe's voice is loud.

"Gabe, be quiet. He'll hear us. What if your mother comes home?"

"Oh, forget it." I hear bedsprings, then look out again.

"What?" She pulls the solar-system quilt I bought Gabe when he was ten over her white body.

"Forget it. I'm not into it anymore," he says with a raised voice and grabs for his underwear, which are at his ankles.

I exhale and look up at the popcorn ceiling and mouth, "Thank you."

"Not into it, or not into me," Darlene says louder, as she roots her shorts out of the quilt with one hand.

The manipulative little . . .

Gabe pulls up his briefs. He looks at Darlene and sighs, "Both." I smile.

Gabe picks up his guitar and starts to strum it.

"Gabe, stop." Darlene puts her hands on the strings. "What did I do? I'm sorry if I hurt your . . ."

"Don't be. It's not you. It's, it's . . ."

"What?" Darlene says.

Gabe stares at the crack in the closet door. I lean back into his clothes.

"Do you remember Mr. Johnson?" I can hear the guitar slide down his body to the floor. Its strings hum. "Crazy Mr. Johnson, the substitute teacher?"

When I look, I see Gabe's quilt fall down her shoulders a bit and Darlene nods.

Gabe is standing in front of her and looks down at the carpet. "'Member his rants about Vietnam?"

"Them damn gooks," she says in a low voice.

"And how our government is as crooked as a rich white man?"

Darlene giggles, then stops suddenly. Gabe is probably giving her the look he gives us when he's in trouble and wants to get out of it. I try not to make a sound.

"Then he would ramble on and on about Agent Orange."

She looks up at him as if praying. "Did he ever lift up his shirt for you guys?"

"Yes. I'll never forget him, those pink and black spots. Mostly, I'll never forget how he described war." I want to laugh at Gabe's performance. "How every muscle in his body was tense. How he could hear every breath he took. How he never really slept at night. How I'm always waiting for something to happen. He knew it was coming, I just don't know what it's going to be or when."

"Gabe, you . . ." Darlene shivers. "Wow, you were really listening."

"This is what it's like." Gabe points to the floor. "What it's like at my house all the time. No, that's not right. There are degrees. Sometimes Mom's too tired or Dad and so not as many dishes get broken."

"That's why all your dishes don't match." Darlene giggles loud then cups her mouth shut.

Darlene has been in the house. She's been here before, and I haven't met her but Sal has. I know why Gabe doesn't want me to meet her. I'd smarten her up. What else are they keeping from me?

Gabe's shoulders drop. "I've been hit a few times."

"Oh." Darlene reaches for his hand.

Gabe takes a step back. He goes for his pants but Darlene leads him to sit on the bed. "Nah, with a flying dish. They only go after each other. Dad would never touch me. I think it's worse when they don't talk to each other because then they talk through us."

"Your sister too?" Darlene's head rolls on to her shoulder.

"Yell, they call us the names they want to call each other. Thing is, you can't dive out of the way like Mr. Johnson did from grenades. It just sucks to hear your dad call your little sister . . . God, Genny." Gabe kicks the frame of his bed with his heel and Darlene jumps.

I try to think of the last time Sal hit Genny. He never touches the girl, and she needs it. Gabe is laying it on thick. Does he do this all the time to get what he wants? I think back to Regie Junior. Genny has mentioned him getting into trouble at school, but not for fighting.

Darlene stands, then takes Gabriel in her arms, folding him into the quilt with her and holding him. His body shakes and Darlene sways. They sway to their own silent beat, until they are in tune with the muffled television commercial coming through the closed door, until they are moving with the rhythm of the cars passing, until they match the hum of the swamp cooler, until they hear a knock on the door, and Gabriel pokes his head out of the quilt.

"Shit," he says.

"Your mom should be coming home soon." I'm grateful he knocked.

So he's done this before.

"All right." Gabe tiptoes to the door and puts his cheek against it. He holds his finger to his lips.

"I think she's at the store," Sal says.

"Yeah, all right," Gabe says.

"Maybe she's at the mandado." Sal's voice gets lower as he walks away from the door. "I want you out of that room, Gabe. Do you hear me?"

41

They are quiet until they no longer hear his steps, and then I hear a flurry of words, movement, and creaking and cling tight to the money in my hand.

"Oh my God. Oh my God. Your father knows. What will he think?" Darlene is standing, pulling on her shorts. "Will he tell your mother? Oh my God."

Gabe puts his arm around her and pulls her head into his chest. "Shhh, shhh. He doesn't know a thing." He kisses her head.

She shakes his touches off and looks on the bed for her bra, spots it, picks it up, slides the straps on, and puts both her arms behind her back to hook it. "Your dad probably thinks I'm a whore."

I nod in the closet.

"No, of course not, he knows you're my girlfriend," Gabe says.

He is still lying to her. Does he ever tell the truth?

"I'm so embarrassed." She closes her eyes as she slips her T-shirt over her head. She lets Gabe stroke her hair.

"You don't have to be embarrassed about my dad, really. He's not worth it." He hugs her.

She pushes him away. "Wouldn't you be embarrassed if my father caught us?"

"My dad didn't catch us." Gabe points to the door.

"Wouldn't you be embarrassed if *my* father did?" She puts her hands on her hips.

"Well, yeah, but you don't have one." His arms flap to his sides.

"You know what I mean." She scans the floor in search of something.

"It's just different with guys."

"How is it different?" She stares at the guitar.

"You're a daughter, and he'd probably shoot me or something."

"He wouldn't own a gun," she laughs.

"Or stab me with one of those arrows you guys have hanging in your hallway. Mine is probably getting drunk right now."

I close my eyes. I wonder if I'm ever going to get out of this closet or this house. How am I going to make it out of here?

"Don't say that." She slaps his bicep.

"Yeah." Gabe rubs his arm where she slapped him. "Sad but true."

"Oh, God." Darlene puts her hands over her eyes and grimaces. "Are you two going to talk about this? Is he going to tell your mother? God, I would die if she knew too."

"Nah, he'd never tell her."

"Why not?" Darlene slips her flip-flops on and strums the guitar with her thumb.

"It's just a guy thing. He just knocked. And we have to get out of here."

"I'm not walking out the front door."

"What, you wanna go out the window?"

I can only see the bed where they have been and I hear the window opening, Darlene giggling and Gabe cussing.

"Hold up, this will only take a minute."

I can see Gabe grab his guitar.

Darlene says, "Wow, now we know why you're drawn to the guitar."

Gabriel laughs. "Yeah, tension."

I hold Gabe's money in one hand and realize I'm tired and I need to stretch.

"We should go." I hear Gabe. "I know a place in the desert."

"No, take me home."

"Yeah, you're right." Gabe sounds heartbroken. "When Mom gets here, they'll start."

"Oh, Gabe. It must be so hard on you."

"Nah, it's not so bad."

"Do you wanna go some place and talk?"

"Can you?" Gabe's voice is hopeful. "Some place we can be alone?"

I don't move. I'm letting this new Gabe settle into my mind. I stay still until I hear the car doors slam, the car start up and drive off. I stand and rub my thighs. I root around the pockets of the jeans he has on wire hangers before I realize I'm stepping on them. I pick up the pack of cigarettes from underfoot, and I throw the shoebox on the floor. I open the door slowly, then shut it behind me and tiptoe out of Gabe's room and down the hallway. I'm thankful Genny went home with Bernie. At least she's still the kid I know. The new Gabe frightens me. Who is he? How long has he been this way? Is it genetic? Did my father's genes skip a generation? How am I going to have the funeral here? How am I going to get through it? I need to get out of here. I need to think.

"Moní? That you?" Sal says. It sounds like he's in the bathroom from the echo. "Gabe?"

I stop in the hallway, then inch toward the front door. I open the door and walk out.

CHAPTER SIX

The Seduction

I GULP THE cold coffee in my hand, then toss the Styrofoam cup behind me. I want more caffeine, no, a drink. The baby seems to stir, but I know it's my nerves. I know the gold room key is at the bottom of my purse. Cigarette smoke is the first thing I smell before I walk into Rocky's. Inside the bar, round tables are crowded with the same padded captain chairs I sat in when Vicente brought me here as a kid. The chairs surround a defeated-looking boxing ring. The two skinny boxers inside the ring dance near its corners, arms dangling. For a minute, I wonder if they are the same boxers from my childhood. But the canvas, now cherry red, snaps me back. It is gray in the center. It used to be electric blue. The black ropes are so worn that the white fiber underneath shines through. Those are probably still the same. I touch my belly and it seems to help quiet the churning. A group of ten people stand near the left-hand corner of the ring, away from the bar. I spot *the one* with a group of men from work, some still wearing their brown shorts. His hair is slicked back and looks wet. I like it better this way. Better than when he comes by the house on deliveries with dry, messy hair. He changed out of his work shorts. Good. I like men better in pants, but the shining polyester print he has on covers his arms. His short-sleeved work shirt shows them off. Those dark jeans are creased to a hard point in the front; not bad. Maybe he'll come inside when he delivers if I introduce myself here. I inhale deep, then walk toward him, trying to remember if he told me it was his brother or his nephew who is a boxer. The smell of stale beer, a faint scent of bleach, and an even fainter scent of vomit make me stop midstride. I fight the nausea. My eyes water and I hold my stomach. I swallow the bitter taste rising up and breathe deep. I curse myself for not forcing the witch's tea down every day. It's still in there. I touch my stomach. It turns flips and I want this to end. My breasts are still tender, and I'm still craving everything. Right now, my craving is physical. I see him, waving his arms to explain something to a group of men and one woman. The red spotlight makes the instruments on the stage look haunted, and the boxing ring looks almost holy under white lights. I straighten up, undo a button on my blouse, and continue on. If Regie doesn't want me, I'll find someone who does. Two women and a man step in my way, but I keep moving. I'm as fearless as the thin boxers inside the boxing ring. I wedge in behind him and bump him. He turns to me.

"Hey!" He looks at my breasts, then right into my eyes.

"Oh, I'm sorry. Did I hurt you? I was trying to get the bartender's attention." I point toward the bartender and feel queasy.

"Yeah." He rubs his shoulder in an exaggerated gesture and cracks a smile.

"Well, then let me buy you a drink," I say. The people surrounding him shout insults at the boxers.

"How about I buy *you* a drink?" He takes a peek at my cleavage. "What are you doing here, Mrs. Montoya?"

I stand on tiptoes to help his view and wave toward the bartender, who ignores me. Why did he have to call me missus? "I got my own cash, really, I can handle this."

"Looks like you got it all under control." He lifts his hand and the barkeep comes right over. "This woman here. Níca, right?"

"Monica," I say.

He smiles. "Mónica here would like to buy me a drink."

"His drinks are bought and paid for, amor." The bartender says while watching the fight.

"Pues, what's a woman to do? I feel awful that I hurt your arm and now I can't even buy you a drink." I put my hand on his shoulder where I had bumped him and he is warm, inviting.

He turns his stool so that he is facing me. "How is Regie?"

"Who?" I laugh and hope I don't look surprised. I inch closer between his open legs.

He lights up. He passes a tightly made stick to me. I pause a second and think about the baby inside me but then take a puff, cough, and pass it back. He laughs.

"Don't you smoke?"

"Not really."

"Not even with Regie?"

"What's with you and Regie?" I wonder why he doesn't mention Sal. "You in love or what?"

"Nothing, I just thought." He straightens his back. "Wanna go get stoned?"

"All right." I follow. I think about leaving but I realize that if he knows Regie, this could work out.

"I've got some of Regie's shit." He sits on the tailgate of a truck.

"Can we change the subject?"

"So come here," he says. He pats his knee, and the cigarette glows orange.

I walk toward him slow. He runs his hand from my leg up to my breast. I back away to avoid the pain and my stomach jumps.

"What's up with you? First you're . . ."

"Oh, hell. I'm sorry." I hug myself. "I'm sorry. Maybe this was a mistake."

"No, it's no mistake," he says. "I'm just not used to this."

"Really?" I laugh. "You mean no one comes on to you in your tight shorts?"

"Oh, yeah, they whistle and act like they're interested in front of their coworkers. But I never get any."

I want to roll my eyes but say, "That's not what I heard."

"What'd you hear?" He inhales deep, then looks up at me, waiting.

"Never mind. I didn't know you knew Regie." I let out a deep breath.

He smiles, then exhales smoke into my face. "Everyone knows Regie." He stubs his cigarette on the tailgate of the pickup he sits on, puts the filter in his pocket, gets up, and puts his warm arms around me. He gives me a long kiss with his thin lips that taste like salt.

"I don't know what your game is, but I'm up for anything."

I take him all in. I can feel his hard, thin body. He smells like sweat and mold. I'm so excited that I bite his lip. He chuckles and bites back. I grope for my purse hanging at my shoulder and he kisses my nose and forehead. I try to distance myself to get a better feel inside the pocket of my bag. "Here, take my key."

His callused fingers dig into my arms. I find the key and hold it up over our heads. He looks up and stares at the key. I want to lick the stubble on his neck. He coughs and drops his hands away from me.

"A key to my hotel. I'm staying at the San Jose. Maybe after the fight you could drop by."

He looks down the street then up at the stars and finally at me; he smiles so that I see every one of his teeth. "You planned this? With me?" He laughs out loud and shakes his head. He slides his hand over my arm, takes the key, and slips it into his jean pocket. With his arm around my waist, he pulls me to him hard, kisses me, rubs his hands down my back, and rests them below my cheeks.

A door opens and someone yells, "Fred's up, guy."

"I gotta go," he whispers. "You'll wait?"

"If I don't you've got my key."

"Right." He puts his hand in his pocket, then takes it out and places his hand on the back of my neck, leading me back into the club. "I've got to watch my nephew." I can feel the roughness of his fingers. I nod and he grips me harder, then lets me go.

Inside the bar, he walks ahead of me and over toward the ring. When he gets to the ring, he whispers something to a man next to him and they both look in my direction. I glance over my shoulder at the bottles of liquor behind the bar. My stomach turns. The bell rings and he watches a short muscular kid in red satin shorts. He yells and shoots punches at an invisible opponent in front of him. He slaps his friend's back next to him and yells some more. I close my eyes and imagine what his rough hands will feel like on my skin. I think about the rough, callused hands moving everywhere. Caressing my butt, back, shoulders, arms, and sides. I'm lost in a daydream but get grounded in reality when I remember my skin. I hope it won't peel tonight. When I open my eyes, Regie is standing in front of me. I blink to make sure he is real. His long hair shines and I want to run my fingers through it. I can smell the rosemary soap he uses, and mint on his breath. I peek over him toward the ring.

"What the fuck are you doing here?" Regie puts his arm around my waist and blocks my view of the ring. "Where's Sal?"

"Probably at home." I try to slip out of his grip. "He hates this place."

"Is he sick?" He slips his other hand around my waist and pulls me so close I can feel his crotch.

"Why are guys so interested in each other?" I lean away from him toward the bar.

"I'm not." He looks back toward the ring and then at who I am watching. "You don't waste time."

I brush my hair away from my shoulder. "You were watching from the back, weren't you?"

He cinches my waist with his fingers. "It's only been a week."

"Five days since you called it off." I shrug my shoulders. "You don't trust me, so I'll find someone who does."

"You think you're tough." He sits on a barstool and lifts me onto his lap.

I jump off, but he catches my arm and makes me face him. I look up. "No, not at all. Why didn't you send word?"

"I was going to." His eyebrows crease and I can tell he's lying. "You know how it is with family. We're cool though, right?

"My son is going to kick Junior's ass if he doesn't lay off," I say.

"¿M'ijo? He doesn't fight anyone but himself. Don't change the subject."

"You ended it. Remember? Too dangerous." I stare into his weak eyes. "Besides, I know you too well."

"What the fuck does that mean?" He looks over at his friend, who is leaning over the bar talking to the bartender, and then at me.

My face flushes, and my eyes tear up. I can't look Regie in the face. I didn't expect this rush of emotion. He rubs one hand across the inside of my thigh and I feel light-headed. He puts his other under my chin and props my face up.

"If we start up, again, every day, like before, we'll get caught . . ." I wonder if I should tell him. What could he do? What would we do? Is this skinny young boy what I want—a dealer with a kid who might be a bully? I feel foolish and old. His touch makes me ache and I push his hand away from my stomach. I have to make something up. He's waiting.

"If we did, we'd fall. I'd fall so deep that I would drown. Drown, you know. And drowning is not something I can afford with Sal and the kids." I hold my belly with both hands and his mouth parts in surprise. I almost smile. I feel him get hard against my thigh and I'm relieved that he believed me. Then he frowns.

He points with his chin toward the ring. "But you'd fuck him?"

I tip my head slightly.

His friend nudges him. "That may be the sweetest blowoff I've ever heard, ese."

"You believe that shit?" He tries to kiss me and I pull away.

I lean back farther and can see the guy is no longer watching his nephew. People are filing into the bar. He stands and stares at me. I step away from Regie's embrace and walk away. I stand a few feet away from Regie and stare at everyone coming in. Mike smiles and looks back at his nephew, who is on the mat.

"I wouldn't let you drown," Regie says.

I want to laugh but walk toward the front door instead, and I know Regie is following me. Why do I feel this way? He loves me. If I told him about the baby, he'd probably leave Sandra. I can't leave Sal, the twins. He'll make life difficult. Hasn't he already? How much longer can this last? Oh, but the kid can last. He doesn't act like a kid when we're alone. Mike won't come tonight. Still, I keep walking. People cheer the boxers on.

Before the door shuts Regie pushes me up against the brick wall outside and kisses me hard. "Get a room," I hear a girl say. She giggles before the door slams. I tangle my fingers in his long hair. The rosemary soothes me. For the first time since I arrived, I don't feel nauseated. I am going to let him do what he wants. I need this. Regie's breath is hot and my back rubs against the brick and throbs. I hold him tight and try to forget everything. He puts his hands inside the back of my pants and works them underneath my underwear and squeezes. I kiss and kiss his thick lips.

"Let's go to my hotel," I say.

"You got a room?" He bites. "What about Mike?"

"We'll be finished before the fight is over." I kiss him hard.

"I can last." Regie pulls away.

"I know. I was talking about me," I say to make him feel good.

He nods and laughs.

For some reason, baths leave me tired, happy, and light. I only take them in hotels. A queen-size bed, minibar, television, and claw-foot bathtub is heaven. I'm glad Regie left. I have this room to myself all night. I can sleep in the middle of the bed. The loud knock on the door startles me.

"Shit," I moan. "Hold on a minute."

I jump up too fast. My head spins and I have to stand still to calm myself. I cinch the belt on my white robe.

"Moníca, it's Mike from the club."

"Oh, Mike, hold on. I fell asleep." I grab my purse from the nightstand and root through it, looking for the purple bottle. When I find it, I spray Dior in the air and on the bed and drop everything on the floor.

"Sure you did," he whispers.

Hurriedly, I open the door.

Here's your key. He points it at me.

"I thought you had forgotten about me." I look at the key and caress his hand.

"No. Maybe I should I have."

I kiss him and blink, then touch my lips. They are sore. He backs me into the room. The smell of Poison is everywhere. It's suffocating. He doesn't seem to notice; he just stares at the rumpled sheets, then he sits on the bed and takes off his shoes like they burn his feet. He unsnaps the buttons on his shirt in one quick motion and frowns at me.

"So, how much do you charge?"

I put my hands over my mouth so he can't see my smile. I clear my throat and act angry. "What? What did you say?"

"How much?" He takes his jacket off, folds it, and lays it next to him.

I step toward him and laugh. "You're free because you're so cute when you're mad." I put my hands on his shoulders and slide a leg over his waist. My robe opens. I feel reckless and alive. "I didn't expect to see Regie."

"What's going on?" He squeezes my thigh.

I grit my teeth and grab hold of the hair on his head. "Nothing you need to worry about."

With one hand he pulls the comforter off the bed and lays me in it. While on top of me, he kicks the quilt to the floor.

"What are you doing?" I undo the belt to the robe.

"I'm not lying where he's been."

I hear the ting of his belt buckle and help him with his fly. "How can you be so sure it was him?" He slaps my hands away and slips his pants and underwear off. He is rock hard and I let out a sigh. "You're huge."

He grins. "Come here. You want some?"

"Yes." He crawls toward my face and slides himself into my sore mouth. I feel his need with every thrust. He stops. Jumps off me like I'm hot. He tears the robe off of me. I laugh and push him away. He doesn't like it and squeezes my face with one hand. I no longer smile, then he thrusts himself into me. I let out a surprised

52

scream and he chuckles. I act scared, make myself tremble, and try to move away. He thrusts harder and laughs out loud. I pretend to struggle, and he groans. This is almost too easy. When he finishes, I scoot away from underneath him, sit on the edge of the bed, and pretend to cry.

"Monica? You okay."

When he touches my shoulder, I heave, and real tears stream down my face. I can't stop them. I don't know what I'm doing here. Why I came. Who is this? I want to go home. I want my father. I want Sal. I want Regie. He wraps me in his arms and holds me. "I'm sorry. Shhh. So sorry," he says.

I'm sorry too, so sorry.

I wake to his snoring. There is no spit in my mouth and I panic. I push his legs off of my naked body and put on the shirt lying next to me. As I feel for buttons, I notice it's his, but I don't care because I'm thirsty. I tiptoe to the bathroom for the ice bucket. I open the hotel room door and peer down the hallway. Not a soul out. I let the door shut behind me and walk toward the elevator.

The elevator door opens, and I drop the silver ice bucket I am holding. Regie walks out carrying his briefcase.

"Why the hell are you still here?" he says. "You need to go."

He steps toward me and fingers the snaps on my shirt. He traps me against the wall between a forearm and his body. His breath is strong with mint and familiar scents of rosemary, pot, and shoe polish. I want him to kiss me and he's about to say something else but he turns to look down the hall.

Mike is standing in front of my room. I call out to him. "Hey." He doesn't look at me. Keeps his eyes on Regie, who is now facing him.

Mike, shirtless, walks toward us and puts out his hand to shake. He is frowning. He towers over Regie. Makes him look like a kid.

I squeeze out from behind Regie and place a hand on Mike's bicep. I tremble. He puffs out his chest and puts his arm around me.

"Qué onda?" Regie takes his hand.

"Where's the ice?" He looks at me.

I point toward the doorway next to the elevators, then bend down to pick up the ice bucket. The elevator door opens and a man with a green tattoo of a lizard or dragon tail that peeks out of his shirt sleeve eyes me. Nervous, I pull the neck to the shirt closed. He pats the pocket to his slacks, which have a large bulge.

I don't move.

"Where you been?" The elevator door closes and he flexes when it hits him. "Is there a problem?" He looks at me and then at Mike.

"Nah, just talking." Regie picks up the briefcase he set down when we met in the hallway. He straightens up and stands in front of me to say something.

"We're waiting." I can hear the man pat the front of his pants again.

Regie looks up quick and steps into the elevator. We watch the doors close and I can hear banging inside. Like someone being thrown against a wall.

I let out a breath, wretch, and throw up.

CHAPTER SEVEN

Unraveled

MY SAND-DRENCHED JEANS chafe the skin on my thighs. I don't care. I'm still taking them off. There seems to bo more dirt in my pants than on the desert floor. I'll worry about the rawness of it tomorrow. Worry about how Regie and I got here. Worry about how he tried to break it off last week. Worry about the bruise over his eye. Worry about the baby. Right now, right now, I only want his body on top of mine. I need it for shade from the after-noon sun, even though the sand burns my skin from the bottom. It's that I don't want to get any darker, and Regie doesn't mind it. Getting darker. He says his brownness is his protection. From what? I wonder, but I don't want to waste time talking. He needs this too; he doesn't want us to end either. My back on this packed dirt, his back against the sky, is the only time I feel free, untouch-able. I trace the bones of his spine with my fingers. It's gritty. The weight of his body reminds me, I'm here, alive. His hair hanging over his shoulders tickling my face, the sand dunes underneath me, his thrusting, the mesa, the heat, it's real. What doesn't seem real is my life—Sal, the kids, this baby inside me.

"Did he make you feel this way, Níca?" Regie stares down at the tangled dark vee where our bodies touch. He pushes. Grunts. "You're crazy for it."

"I can't help it." I hiss and stab at the hot red sand on either side of me. Its sting turns me on.

"You fuck him in . . . shit, here they come." Regie pulls out so quick I don't have time to think. My oasis vanishes. He gets to his feet, kicking up sand. It settles on my crotch. "I knew this would fucking happen. I fucking knew it. This is why I can't do this anymore." He lifts his pants over his thin hips and snaps the button, forgetting his fly. He doesn't bother dusting himself off. He walks up the embankment to the trunk of the car before the other car I hear heading toward us parks. "Stay there. Got it? Why don't I learn? Don't fucking move or say a word!"

Blinded by Regie's quick good-bye, I'm still. A few seconds pass before I bend my neck up to look overhead. I can see the driver's side door and Regie's profile as he opens the trunk. He's all Indio just like Vicente. I wonder if I'm far enough down the sand dune. I should be at the base. If they saw me, here, with Regie at work . . . I don't want to think about it. Maybe I shouldn't have walked by his house. I knew he'd be outside fixing an old toaster or TV set. He likes old things. Besides, it's too hot to be inside without an air conditioner. I wanted to talk to him about Regie Junior. The little bully he's raising. When I saw him, everything I planned to say changed. When he told me Sandra didn't get off work until six o'clock, I knew we only had several hours together. All he said was "wetback fuck," and I left with him. I should have kept walking. I should have reminded him about his bullshit breakup. Yeah, maybe I will remind him and give him my big surprise. I don't see him anymore—I only hear him and I'm not moving. I'm baking but my back and butt already cooled the sand below me, thank God. I wish I had some clothes on. If I move even an inch, it'll burn and I'll have to wait for my body to adjust to the heat again. I lie and wait, don't even brush the dirt off my pelvis, my breasts already itching.

"Órale." I hear Regie.

A man's low voice says, "What were you doing back there? Jacking off?"

I hear laughter, not Regie's, then silence, a very long silence. I panic and think about burying myself in the sand.

"Nah, I was just taking a shit," he says.

"This whole fucking place is a toilet," the low voice says. "You got me hooked up?"

"Don't I always?" I can tell Regie is smiling by the way his voice gets whispery.

I can hear the metal latches click in the quiet, and I smile because Regie thinks that that black briefcase makes him look professional.

"That's what I'm talking about," another higher voice says.

"¿Y lo mío?" Regie wants to know.

"Sapos gots it for you," the high voice says.

A door opens and slams, and I put my fingers in my ears, expecting the worst. I look to my right and see my bra and underwear up the dune about ten steps away. My jeans and shirt are close by, thank God.

"All ready, man," Regie says, and I take my fingers out. "Laters." Then the familiar three knocks on the car like he does.

"I gotta take a piss," the one they called Sapos says. "I'm outta tallboys." His voice is getting louder and I sit up. "We're gonna have to go back—"

"Híjole, bro. I wouldn't drain it over there. I did some damage," Regie says.

"You know where they sell cold ones?" Sapos's voice sounds farther away. "I mean the iced-down ones, not that refrigerated bullshit."

I put my hand over my racing heart, look at the blue sky, and whisper "thank you."

Regie says, "Yeah, Howdy's on Montana, that's where I get mine."

"Hey, Johnny, we need—"

"Yeah, yeah, Howdy's. I'm not deaf, pendejo," Johnny's high-sounding voice says even higher.

"Get in the car. We've got more business to take care of," the low voice says. A car door slams and the tires crackle over the sand. "Your fly."

Regie laughs and I hear them drive away. I tilt my head back and look above me. I see Regie's profile again as he puts his brief-case in the trunk and throws a black duffle bag in next.

I get up and dust myself off. Grab my T-shirt and jeans. I don't bother going after my underwear or bra, because Regie threw them too far across the embankment, and I don't feel like crawling after them. My feet slip in the sand and the climb is difficult, but I reach the car and stand, shield my eyes with a hand to see the white Cadillac driving off in the distance. Regie slams the trunk shut, runs at me, and shoves me to the ground.

"What the fuck is wrong with you?" He stands over me and looks the opposite direction. "Do you know what they'll do if they think I have someone else with me? Jesus, Níca, you're going to get us killed. Stay there. Don't move."

On the ground, I pull on my jeans, rough and angry. I inspect my white T-shirt, which is tinged orange from my falling on top of it. Regie keeps standing next to the driver-side door and looking toward the car. After a few seconds, he opens the car door and gives me his hand. I take it. When I'm next to him, he slaps my butt and a cloud of dust forms. He bows and opens the door. I crawl inside holding my T-shirt and slide across the seat, and he gets in behind me, then starts up the engine.

"I'm sorry." I dust off my shirt.

He doesn't say anything, just looks at my breasts and keeps his hand on the gearshift at my side. He looks past me out the passenger-side window at the trail of dust in the distance, then at me. "Loca, you're starting to burn." He rubs a soft finger over the skin of my shoulder.

"You think we should stay here until dark?" I cough through the cloud of dust in the car.

"Don't you gotta get home to Sally?" He blows air in his mouth so that his cheeks fill up.

I don't laugh at his imitation of Sal.

He exhales. "Como lo quieres, I'll leave your ass here."

"You would." I shrug his touch off. "Turn on the air, will you?" I touch the knobs on the dash but he slaps my hands away.

"Hold up, yeah?" He revs the engine and I turn on the air.

"Let's go." I pull down the visor to look at my sunburn.

"No, we've got to wait at least ten more minutes to be sure they're gone and not waiting. I'm not sure if they saw you or not. I can see the dust from their car the entire seven miles. I know what it looks like and how long it lasts, that's why I always meet out here."

"I get it." I snap the visor shut.

"Yeah, you did. Didn't you, cochina?" Regie pinches my left nipple, and I suck air and slap his hand away. He rubs his hand and laughs. "You want to finish what you started?" He strokes my dusty hair and forces my head down toward his crotch. I let him, because I know he's scared. I also know Regie's dick is as raw as I am. It's the sand and the sun. Still, I'm burned and satisfied.

"I love you," he says afterward but doesn't kiss me. "But do me a favor, yeah? If you want to see me don't fuck someone else or send your kid to beat up mine." He buttons his pants, forgets the zipper, and puts the car in drive. The sand crackles beneath the tires as I slip on my shirt.

"I get that boys are boys," he says as he drives slow. "But my kid's a runt. He's in high school and he looks like an eight year-old, like I did. That Gabe, he's already growing a beard. He's as big as Sal."

I open my mouth but shut it. Regie Junior is small. I hold my belly until we are on the paved road.

Regie leans back, far back, in his seat and his forearm drapes over the steering wheel. I can't help but think of how careless he is, can be. He should have never let me come with him here. This is dangerous for me, for us. I fumble with my heels on the floorboard.

"My kid? Yours started it. I just told Gabe to put an end to it." I cinch the leather strap, sit up, and pull my seat belt so fast it burns the skin on my arm. "Ouch."

"You really do live in your own world." Regie shifts in his seat. "How's my carnal, Sally?"

I sigh and let that go. "He's fine. He's not your friend."

"What? He's fat?"

"Very funny. He's fine." I cross my arms. "He's on a diet."

"What happens to us when we get married, Nina?" Regie pushes in a cassette tape. Steven Tyler sings "Dream On." "Why do we stop living?"

"It doesn't happen to everybody." Outside, gray jackrabbits zigzag into weeds.

"Look at you, you're hot. Shit, hotter than my twenty-five-year-old wife. What are you, thirty-five? Why'd you marry *him*?"

I look at the floorboard to hide my smile and talk slow. "Forty-five. Because I knew he could take care of me, and that he would never leave me like my father. Never . . ."

"Shit, I can take care of you." He hits the steering wheel.

I laugh too fast, too loud, and Regie slaps me with a look.

"Nah, all I'm good for is a laugh and a fuck." Regie white knuckles the wheel.

My face heats up and I play with the silver lock on the door as the weeds on the side of the road give way to billboards outside. I don't know where to even begin. There is too much to say, so much I have to say. "I've never understood why we get just one partner. I don't get it, never have. I mean, it's such a natural function—sex. It's like eating. Why can't we sample different people? We get so caught up in loving and owning each other. For what? We're all gonna die. If I didn't have to get married, I never would have." The lechuguilla in the median bends in the wind. Regie is looking straight ahead and hasn't moved and doesn't even sing along to the music.

"Your old man's philosophy?" He grabs a pack of cigarettes from the dash and hands me the lighter, then slinks lower in his seat.

I light him up as we speed past junkyards. "Don't ever compare me to that dead two-timing asshole."

"Sal cheated?" He flips his hair and glances at me. "I never knew he had it in him."

"No. Never." I shake my head, then nod. We pass a green sign that reads El Paso. "Yes, I thought you were talking about my—oh, never mind."

He sighs. "Yeah, I heard stories about your old man. Got invited to his funeral too."

"It's not a funeral." I slap my thighs. A dust cloud forms. "Vicente's been dead for years, and we're just going to divide his ashes. Who invited you?"

"Who do you think?" His white teeth shine.

"Damn, Bernie." I pull down the overhead visor and look at my crow's-feet in the credit card–sized mirror.

"No, Cheno. He knows Bernie's uncle. He knows all the Gomezes."

I wonder if Sal's brother knows about us. About this. "Damn, Cheno knows everyone." I slam the visor shut.

"And everything." Regie drums his thumbs on the steering wheel and stares straight ahead.

I wonder if he's told my brother-in-law anything. I focus on Regie's profile, searching for a clue. He is beautiful—smooth, dark skin, sharp cheekbones, and big, full lips. "You and Cheno still pal around?"

"I need to stay straight. One fuckup and I'm out." Regie pushes his hair back away from his face like a girl. "Nah, he's too much trouble. Talks too much."

I giggle. "Tell me about it."

"So why'd you invite him to the funeral, then?"

"It's not a— oh, never mind. I guess Sal did. He's family."

"You're such a good wife."

We drive in silence.

"They need to get these people off the mediums." Regie points toward the windshield.

I watch a homeless man with no leg. "Medians."

"You hungry?" Regie reaches for my stomach.

I slap his hand away. "No."

He pulls into a parking lot so fast I have to hold the door handle to keep from falling on his lap. "I'm hungry. Let's go to Chico's."

I scan the parking lot for cars I recognize. He *is* reckless. "I hate this one. It's so dirty."

"So don't eat." Regie parks and jumps out of the car. He waits with the door open for me to unbuckle my seat belt and slide over to the driver's seat to get out. "I guess you're full, huh, chula." He tries to grab for my nipple. I slap his fingers hard. "I just need to get some money." He walks to the trunk and opens it while I look inside through the tall windows, scanning faces, before I shut the car door. "Vamos?" He points to the restaurant, slams the trunk, and we walk inside. Regie holds the door open for me and an elderly woman, who is with her grandson. Inside, Vicente Fernandez's tenor booms out of the jukebox.

"I want a single and a limonada." I walk toward the corner of the place.

"It's not fresh."

I stop. "Yeah, right, a Sprite then."

"No fries? You gotta have fries."

"No," I say, looking at Regie and the five others in line in front of him. I don't think I can stomach the rolled tacos drowned in orange sauce.

There are only two open tables in the restaurant, and I head for the corner table at the same time as the young boy we walked in with does. He turns and looks at me, and I size him up too. I am closer to the table, and he knows this because he looks toward the other open table near the jukebox. I am halfway there when he decides to make a run for my table. I sit too fast, and my forearms stick to the fake wood laminate. The boy stands in front of me, snaps his fingers, and gives me a toothless smile. He reminds me of Gabe when he was six. I watch Regie place the order. He is going to get me killed if I keep this up. I am thankful this place is fast. We can get in and out of here in no time. He's trying to impress the cashier, taking out the entire roll of bills to pay. Now he looks like a lost schoolboy searching for me. He's careless and dangerous, like Vicente was with our lives. My cheeks are hot.

"What's wrong with you?" He sits in the booth, his back toward the other tables. "You sick?"

"I can't stand him." I make a fist ready to punch someone and surprise myself. I have never said that about Vicente out loud.

"Who?" Regie looks behind him as he sits.

"Vicente, who else?" I think about throwing his ashes in the toilet.

Regie pushes his hair behind his shoulders. "How can you hate the most beloved singer of all time?"

"Numero veinte ocho?" sounds over the loudspeaker.

He checks the white slip of paper before he mewls like a cat in heat. "Las distancias apartan las ciudades / las ciudades destruyen las costumbres."

I laugh when I realize Vicente Fernandez is on the jukebox but I don't correct Regie. I sing out of the side of my mouth, "Te dije adios y pediste que nunca / que nunca olvidara . . ." I stop singing when I realize I'm singing the same line my father sang when I would sit on his lap as a girl. Regie's thick black brows crease and he turns to scan the room for the reason I stopped. We both spot two men walking inside. We watch them head toward an empty table filled with paper plates and cups. Regie grips the table like he is about to get up when one of the men nods slightly and says, "Estamos bien, bro." The low voice is the same one I heard at Red Sands, and I notice the lizard-tall tattoo poking out of the other man's T-shirt sleeve. Regie loosens his grip, gives a nod back, and looks at me. His face is pale. His knee bumps the table and his leg doesn't stop shaking. I don't say a word, and I give a silent prayer. I hope they don't notice the orange tinge of my T-shirt, and I wonder if the tattooed one remembers me from the hotel. When I peer over Regie's shoulder at the men, the lizard-tattooed man glares at me, and I shift my gaze to Regie.

I raise my voice and try to sound relaxed. "I don't know what the hell people see in him. He can't act either. My father loved him. Why?"

Regie shakes his head hard and tries to act natural, but his knee is still banging underneath the tabletop. "No. You got it all wrong. I love the sex scenes in Chente's movies."

"You mean the rape scenes." I look only at Regie.

"What?" He blows his hair out of his eyes and tries not to look out the corners toward the men.

"I'm supposed to buy that after Chente rapes a young girl, someone as old as Genny, that the kid is going to fall in love with the guy that forced her. That's what happens in every one of his movies." I slap the table and it echoes so that the men look up. I duck my head, not wanting them to see my face.

"Isn't that how it is with you women? No means yes, que no?" Regie scratches his nose and hair falls in his face. "You don't know what you want. He remind you of your old man?"

Disgusted and frightened, I pull my forearms off the table. "Dirty." I think about how stupid this is. How reckless. How I should tell him about the pregnancy but can't now with this. I wave away a fly next to my arm. It lands on the edge of the paper boat dish of someone's leftover tacos two tables over, walks on the grease, then sinks into the orange liquid. "I followed him across the bridge when I was a teenager." I can't look up because I know that Regie meant Sal. "I got his address from his wallet. Memorized it. He lived in a nice fraccionamento with his real family. I had the taxi park a few houses away and we watched Bernie and her little sister Graciela run in and out of the house. Their house had a door like the one at my mother's."

"I . . . I meant Sal." Regie folds and unfolds the slip of paper with his order number. He stares at it like it's written in Spanish. "I don't know what I would've done. You ever tell your mother you saw them?"

"No." I look into his alert eyes. "What are *we* doing, Regie?"

Regie shrugs and his knee stops banging the table. "We're trying to stay alive or saving a place in hell for ourselves."

"You don't even go to church." I touch his hands.

"Numero veinte nueve," comes over the loudspeaker.

He puts his hair behind his ears before he gets up to get our food. "I know, but my abuela does and she tells me all about it. What we're doing is a carnal sin."

"Mortal," I say, but Regie is gone. I'll bet there is a special place in hell for what I'm trying to do with this thing. Sometimes I wish I were Catholic and the decision would be made for me. I pat my belly, and I look over at the men. The tattooed man blows me a kiss. I look away and they both laugh.

"What are they laughing at?" Regie whispers as he puts the tray down.

"I dunno." I hug myself.

Regie smiles too and looks over at the men, then smiles wide. They stop laughing. He whispers, "Eat fast and let's get the hell out of here."

I take my tacos off the plastic orange tray. Regie eats quick before the bottom of his paper bowl turns to mush. I look at Regie and smile when I hear, "Volver, Volver, Volver" boom out of the jukebox.

Under my breath I say, "No one can sing a ranchera like Jose Alfredo. He's got talent and class. The only reason Vicente Fernandez is so popular is because all the good charros are dead. He owes his career to someone else's misfortune."

"Kinda like Sal."

"Lookit those assholes," I whisper and nod toward the men. Regie's cue ball–sized eyes and tense muscles tell me he got the message. "He got his job like anyone would. Showed up, said the right things—"

"Kissed the right asses." Regie peeks out of the corner of his eye at the men before he says, "It would have been mine. He took out Davidson's daughter. You know?"

"I don't want to hear this." I drop my plastic fork into my bowl and orange liquid splashes onto the table.

"You need to, so you'll know what you married."

The men sit across from each other on the edge of the booth, legs spread wide, one arm draped across the table, the other wrapped around the back of the booth, watching the people walk by and listening to every word we say.

"Numero cinquenta uno," sounds over the loud speaker.

The tattooed man gets up, and as he passes our table he winks at me. Regie doesn't see. I pick up the white plastic fork and stab at the rolled taco but can't penetrate it. The fork breaks. Regie gets up. I stop stabbing at the taco and hold my breath. He is too reckless. When he walks past the man, I blow it out. I don't look over their way this time. Regie comes back with two plastic forks, sits down, and shakes his head. The men are walking out the door with a white bag and two drinks in large red-and-white cups.

"You trying to get me, us, killed?" He hands me a fork and watches the men from our seat next to the window get into a black Bronco outside. He drapes an arm around the seat of the booth and sinks low, like he's riding his car.

I whisper, "I know exactly who I married. Exactly. Someone who can get up every morning and go into the factory and work day in and day out. Who comes home every night. Can do the job. Provide for a family. Someone who isn't careless."

"I take care of my family." His face is red.

"That's why you don't have an air conditioner."

"Sandra doesn't want one." He leans toward me. "She's all Mexicana. Says she can't breathe with the air blowing on her. They didn't even talk to me, Níca. They just turned me away there in that fake living room attached to the plant. Sal was in there with them, interviewing just like me."

"So, what? You're getting back at him by fucking his wife?" I lean into the table and pronounce all the words slow and clear. "Is that what this is, Regie?"

"Maybe." Regie looks down at his paper bowl. "No. We can't do this no more. It's too dangerous. I'm serious, Níca."

I use my fork to try to drown my taco in its juice. The taco is hard. I stop trying to dunk it and pick it up with my fingers and take a bite. It crunches and juice dribbles down my chin. As I chew I feel the sand between my teeth and remember Ana's tea. I'm going to drink it the right way, keep it down this time, and let it get into my system. I've decided what to do, what's right. I can't do this to Gabe, Genny, Sal. I won't. If I have this baby, I'll unravel like the taco Regie's eating.

CHAPTER EIGHT

La Ofrenda

POINTING TO THE porcelain figurine on the corner shelf, I ask, "Why am I seeing a horse's ass? Why is the grass dead?"

"Qué le vale la madre St. George." Bernie throws a hand up in the air. "He hasn't helped me, why should I feed him or his caballo?"

"You're punishing the horse?" I laugh. "We need to talk about Vicente's ashes, the ceremony."

"You need to talk to your daughter, stop introducing her to men, and think about your sister." Bernie points to herself and flicks her fingers at the St. George statuette. "Jorge's failed me. Otra vez. And I'm sick of watering the zacate for his pinche horse."

"You don't mean that, Bernie." I sit down on the ottoman, where Bernie's feet rest, and put my hands between my knees. I pray for Regie. I need to tell Bernie about last night in case Sal or the kids ask.

"I do." Bernie lifts her feet and places them on the floor, collecting strands of white hair off the fabric on the black velour couch.

"I saw Regie," I say. I don't dare tell her everything.

Bernie picks at the couch like she's taking lice off someone's head. "I'm sick of being good. What does it get me, Monica? More cats—I have three, ya." She makes a fist with the collection of hair in her hands and slams it on the armrest of the black couch.

Stinky, the white Persian lying along the back of the sofa, has a bored expression.

"You love your cats." I swallow hard and eye the black cat asleep on the television set. Here we go—Bernie the sufrida. Wonder how long it'll take. Maybe if I were Catholic like Bernie, I wouldn't do these things.

"No, I don't. Me van a comer when I die, here alone in my house. That's the thanks I'll get. At least I'll be good for someone." She waves the cat off and gets a cold, careless stare in return.

"I've heard of dogs eating their owners." I pet the calico that is rubbing itself against her shins. "Who is this? A new one?"

"You see, not even the pinche gatos are loyal." Bernie stands and the calico runs away. She walks over to the plastic curio cabinet in the corner. She picks up St. George. "Well, I'm sick and tired, sick and tired of those dogs out there. I should just be heartless and selfish like you."

"I'm not . . ." I remember last night and get up. I take St. George and his horse away from Bernadette. The patch of grass St. George's horse has stood on since I've known her is yellow. How long does it take grass to die? How long has she been feeling this way? "You can't be."

"You, you cállate." Bernie walks to the television, hisses at Mancha, who continues sleeping, then picks up the remote control next to him and points it at me. "Everyone wants you." The television lights up and Oprah Winfrey is crying. "You don't know what it's like. I sit here in my home solita, cada noche and watch you abuse the one man, el hombre, el que te ama mas que . . ."

I look at St. George and shake my head, sit down and stare at a silent Oprah, who is being hugged by another black woman. Bernie's so simple. I wish I were more like her.

"You're too stupid to see it, to see him for what he really is, just a man, a man in love trying to make it through this life, like us." Bernie squeezes the remote between her hand and her breast and the channel changes.

It's too early for this. I watch a blonde woman with red lips mouthing words, and then a dark-skinned, pock-faced man walk handcuffed into a brick building. "If you like him so much you can have him."

"You see, you see how stupid you are? You don't see what I'm telling you. I don't want him. I want what you have, what you're too tonta to see. He loves you. His love is what keeps you steady. He's what you're trying to get from all these narcotraficantes."

"Quit exaggerating. He's just a dealer. Small time." I squeeze my legs together and tuck my hands between my legs. I just want to talk about last night. I want Bernie to absolve me of my sins like she always does. I want my father's face explaining to me that I am . . . that what I feel is okay.

"You're dying, Mónica."

"So are you! And what do you have to show for it? Two, three cats now, and this house, this mausoleum?"

"This is a good house."

"This is a house of heartbreak. I hate this house. You don't know what it's like to not have a father. To have a man who leaves at the end of every week to go back to his real family."

"How many days was he here?" She points to the floor.

I count on my fingers. "Three, sometimes four days."

She holds up two fingers and says, "We saw him two days out of the week, dos dias every week, sometimes once a month."

I fold my arms and think of Ana Jurado and then remember the other women I'd seen hug him a little too long at the grocery stores or at restaurants.

"We're all dying and you're going to have to face it. Your, our Vicente era mal, the best thing he gave us." She holds out her hands toward me. "We got the best of him."

I push them away and stand. "No, he wasn't. He loved us all. He loved too much, that was his biggest problem. He wanted to love everybody."

"That's how stupid you are. How much you don't see." She points her index finger and throws up her hands in exasperation.

"I know you think I'm stupid, simple. Sometimes I am. He had two lives, Moníca—two. We weren't enough for him."

"Only two? You sure?" I pout. "He wasn't a bad man. He loved us."

"You're just like him and for that I am thankful." She taps the remote control on her knee. "I thank God every single day that he died."

I sit down. I can't believe how much hate she has for him. And he was her father, her real father. He would still be here if he hadn't wrecked the van, if someone had driven him across to us. His driving was awful.

"My santo has failed me, failed me like my father did, and I'm sick of hoping for a man to rescue me." Bernie sits too, with the remote control clutched to her breasts, and she sighs. "The only strength I've ever gotten was from women. I'm going to become a manflora. Get some respect."

Bernie stands, walks to the door, and grabs her keys hanging off an elephant's trunk glued to the wall near the doorway; it's been there since I was little girl, only it had tusks then. "I have to get out of here."

"Where the fuck you going?" I am up too.

"¿Y a ti qué te importe?" She turns to look at me.

I don't want her to go. I put out a hand. "I need the remote."

Bernie looks in her hand and shakes her head, then throws it at the couch. I don't move. "To drink. You can come if you want or not." Bernie opens the door and walks out.

I let out a breath, grab the remote, and point it at the television. The screen goes black and I rush to the door—and I push over the agave that stuck me.

As Bernie opens the door to the driver's side, I jump in like I used to with Vicente. It seems so natural. When she shuts the door, there is silence. We don't move. I can smell the faint pine scent from the cardboard tree hanging on the rearview mirror. Her breathing gets deeper and the car starts to shake and then there's laughter. The laughter becomes hiccups from both of us, and then quiet, panting relief. I am trembling. Bernie rubs my arm like I am cold and I lean into her.

"I'd make a good bike, qué no?" She winks.

"The kids can call you Uncle Bernadette," I laugh, then I plant a kiss on Bernie's hot cheek. "It's dyke."

She starts up the Road Runner, lets it idle for a minute, and then backs out of the driveway. The tires squeal as she accelerates down the street.

"Ah su manos, you hear the tires?"

"No."

"I did, and I need air for them." Bernie turns on Alameda Drive. I point. "So stop here. Joe will do it for you. He's a cute güero who works here, a little greñudo but good looking."

"I never stop here. I like to do stuff myself. I have two good arms."

"Maybe that's your problem." I squeeze Bernie's arm.

"Yes, I need to think like you. How many men were you with last night?" She shakes my touch off. "I was home alone. I watched the Juan Gabriel concert."

I hold up one finger, and Bernie looks at my finger, smiles, then makes a sharp left turn into the gas station. The tires squeal.

"Güero, I don't know." Bernie watches the tall, slender man with a ponytail get up from a chair and walk toward the car. "I don't like güeros, but I know how to handle them. Watch."

I giggle.

"Nice ride." The attendant, whose name, Keith, is stitched in red above his shirt pocket, walks around the back of the car like he's going to kick the tires. "Gas you up?"

Bernie blushes. "No, no, I don't need gas. I need wind for my llanters."

I put a hand over my mouth to stifle a laugh. "I'm watching and there's not much to see," I whisper, then I lean over Bernie and say, "Can you check under the hood for us?"

Bernie leans forward too and smashes her large breasts with her arms so that they are nearly under her chin. "Jes, jes, please, I think my oil is out."

He puts both hands on her window and leans in and looks only at Bernie. "If you pop your hood for me, I'll take look inside and fix you right up. You also need air in your tires. I could hear you coming in."

Bernie giggles and fumbles for the latch near her knee. Her brown hair grazes Keith's knuckles, and he inhales deep before standing straight and going to the front of the car.

"Jes keep talking, I shink he likes your accent," I tease.

"Cállate. Pinche gabacho pelado. I know my tires squeak, that's what I told him when I got here."

"Pero you know how to espeak him."

"Well, maybe I'm not fluent like you, but I've fucked a güero before. His dick was small, but I got on top y me acabé."

I laugh so loud Keith pops his head out and looks right at me before his head disappears behind the raised hood again.

"Are you drunk?" I say.

"Yes. No, that's where we are going."

"Maybe you're just a little?" I point and Bernie smiles. "Lookit. Is he flexing his muscles? I think he likes you, Bernie."

"Ah sí, he's just . . . hay viene."

Keith walks over to Bernie's window and leans in close. "You're low on oil. You want me to fill her up?"

"Sí, sure, sure, go head."

"I like your accent, Sweetie," he says. "Where you from?"

"El Paso."

"Yeah, I guessed that. I mean originally. Monterrey? Saltillo?"

"No, Juárez."

"Damn, I would have guessed Saltillo with your accent. I'm usually pretty good."

"Well, I was born in Arteaga. I lived there until I was seven. You know it?"

I am quiet. Waiting to hear more. I had no idea she lived in Arteaga. They lived there. She is seven years older, and I realize I don't really know this woman or Vicente's life before us.

"Not well. I visited once or twice, had friends who owned a little house near the plaza."

"Oh, sí, San Antonio de las Alazanas. I'm sure Señor Esteban still sells ajo there every Sunday."

"Uh, ajo?"

"The onion. No, no, how do you call it? Garlic."

"Oh, garlic." He wipes his brow with a forearm and his too-small shirt lifts at the belly and I can see a line of blonde curly hair above the button of his pants. "No one likes full-service stations anymore. They're too old fashioned."

Bernie stares at the hairline too. "I love them. You get to talk to people."

I pinch her hard enough to leave a welt on her arm but she doesn't flinch.

"Let me get the tires."

Bernie turns to me slow, as if in a daze. "Why'd you pinch me?"

"You loooove full-service stations?" I shake my head.

"I do." She looks out the rearview mirror at the attendant. "Now."

"What's up with your English? It's not that bad." I slap her thigh. "Do something about it, now."

Bernie starts the car. "I can't."

"Whoa, whoa," Keith yells. "What's your hurry? I still have one more tire to go. You paying cash? Gonna need a receipt?"

Bernie smiles, turns the car off. "Sorry. Sí, sí, please."

"What the hell are you waiting for? You have to put yourself out there. I do it all the time."

"But you look like that." Bernie points to my face. "And I look like . . ."

I put my face next to hers and move the rearview mirror around until I can see us both in it. "You look like a hot Mexicana to this gabacho. You have those hazel eyes and that alone will get you into anyone's bed."

Bernie looks at her eyes in the rectangular mirror and smiles. She crosses her eyes.

"Hasta la vista, bizca," I laugh.

"I don't want to get into his bed."

"Yes you do. Stop lying to yourself." I fluff her hair.

"I will if you will." She stares right back at me in the mirror.

I stop fluffing her hair, flick her ear, then move away and look out the window, hugging my middle and sighing. I undo the button on my jeans and watch my stomach pooch out. "Shut up."

"Be right back with a total and a receipt," he yells.

Bernie sighs, opens her door, and steps out. I watch her back. She falls in line behind a mother pushing a stroller and two children running toward the doorway to the gas station. The mother fumbles for change in her pocket as the boy and girl charge the gas station door. Bernie waits behind the mother to enter. The mother turns to Bernie and hands her something, then points to the child in the stroller.

Bernie's voice is loud. "Sí, sí, como no."

Bernie walks through the door and seems to fill up the closet-sized room. I can hear the bell ring and I watch, envious, as Keith looks up from behind the counter and smiles wide.

Bernie talks to the children, who have their faces pressed against the vending machine. She hands them something, then walks toward the counter. I laugh because the boy and girl are pushing each other to put their money in the machine first. The boy pushes his sister hard. I watch helpless as the girl falls back and nearly knocks over the oil display in the shape of a pyramid. I relax and smile when I see Bernie between the two. She lets the girl put her money in first before heading back to Keith. I don't see the girl anymore. Bernie walks back toward the machine and kneels. Then I see Bernie fall backward and the oil display tumble down.

"Holy shit." I open the car door and run inside.

I pass the mom, who has her back to the scene while she feeds the baby, then I walk inside where Bernie is covering the girl. The little boy has plastered himself against the wall of the counter where Keith stands. Silver cans litter the small room.

"I'm sorry," Bernie says.

"Hey, no, don't worry. It's not big deal. Are you okay? Are you two okay?" Keith doesn't know how to get to her with the cans on the floor so he hovers near the cash register.

The girl pops up, tiptoes around the cans, and runs out the door, afraid she is in trouble. Her brother runs on tiptoes across the sea of silver and is out the door too.

"All your work," Bernie snorts. "I'm an uncompetent fool."

"Fool? You? No, next time I'll use pallets. Are you sure you're okay? Those cans are heavy." He makes his way to Bernie.

"Uncompetent." Bernie uses the window behind her to get up and I give her my arm but she takes his.

"I'll redo it. I've got a lot of free time anyway. I needed to do something different."

He lifts her up quickly and she is blushing and looking at the mess.

"Are you sure you're okay? I know you're going to have bruises for sure. Those kids come in here every day and every day I wonder when they're going to knock over the display. They need to keep their thieving little hands out of the vending machine."

"No era, ah, it wasn't their fault." Bernie steps over the cans and reaches for the door to leave.

I open the door.

"Hold on, don't you want your credit card?" He holds out a hand toward her and looks at his cash register.

Bernie storms out of the station and I have to jog to keep up. She walks around the car and starts it before I even open the door. "What's wrong with you? Did you get his phone number at least?"

"No. Vámonos."

"What's wrong?"

"Señorita Gomez? Miss Gomez? Wait up. You forgot your credit card. The gas—" Keith yells just as I shut my door.

She puts the car in drive, and he has a long muscular arm on her half-open window. His greasy fingers leave smudges on the glass.

"Miss Gomez? You forgot this. You sure you're okay? I mean those cans hit you pretty hard."

"What happened?" I look at him and see the dark-brown strand of hair jutting out of his right nostril that curves all the way inside the next one.

"Miss Gomez is covering for the thieving brats," he says.

"Thieving? Como ladrón." Bernie looks at me and I nod.

"She was trying to rip me off." He looks over the way the family came.

"Steal? She paid money. Put money into the ancient machine of yours." Bernie stares at him.

I notice that his arms are sinewy and not all muscular, and his long brown hair only looks blonde because of all the split ends. Bernie pulls the credit card out of his hand and drives off.

"Why did you leave? He was about to ask you out." I look back and see him walking toward the office, shaking his head.

"You want me to go out with a racist pendejo?" She waves a hand in the air. "Didn't you hear him?"

"Well, yeah, but you were just complaining about how you didn't want to be alone. He's not racist. Please, Bernie. He's just pissed because he has a lot of work to do."

"I'd rather be alone than with someone like that."

"He was good looking."

She shakes her head as she comes to a complete stop behind a truck filled with saplings, grass, manure, and shovels. "I better get home. I need to water the grass."

"Too late, your patch is already dead." As the truck takes off, two squares of turf fall off a pallet on the truck.

We both look at each other then at the street.

"A gift straight from God's hands for my santo. Get out, get out, hurry, get the grass."

I do what she says, pick up both squares of turf in front of the car, and walk toward the back of her car. She is out the door and opening the trunk. "St. Augustine. It's St. Augustine—the best kind. God is watching over me."

"If he was watching over you, here, in the desert, the truck would have been filled with sand. This," I throw the waterlogged squares into the open truck with a grunt, "is just another example of God's cruelty."

CHAPTER NINE

Not What It Seems

I'M GLAD BERNIE didn't want to go drinking and dropped me off
or I would have missed his call. Barefoot, I pace the Saltillo tile
that Sal put in himself. I suck air when I step on the sharp edge.
I hold on to the sink with one hand and rub the sole of my foot
with the other. What's keeping him? What's so important that he
needs to come home in the middle of the afternoon? Did Sal find
out about last night? About Regie? Mike? He's probably just mad
that I didn't come home. I pick up a dishcloth in the sink and
head to the refrigerator. Might as well do something while I wait.
I use my fingers to pry the seal of the refrigerator door open
because the handle is long gone. I can't remember if it was me or
Sal who kicked it off.

"Ouch." I hit my head on the shelf above. "Don't sneak up on
me like that!"

"I don't sneak. That's for you and the kids." He steps away and
pulls a stool out from under the counter he built. "I just walked in
like I always do."

I let the cool air hit me a few seconds longer before I get up
from kneeling and shut the refrigerator door. His shoulders are
drooping like they did when he told me about my mother's death.
I'm not sure I'm ready to hear what's he has to say.

"You hungry?" I open the kitchen drawer. "I could cook you
something?"

"Nah, I ate already."

"Coffee? I could make some, or chocolate?"

"No, Monίca, I don't want anything." He slaps his hand hard on the counter top as he sits on the stool.

"Okay, then." I stand in the middle of the kitchen and touch my stomach. I hope it's not what I think. "What is it? I told you I fell asleep at Bernie's watching Juan Gabriel again."

Sal doesn't look at me. He is concentrating on the tile counter top he built. "I was only flirting. Kidding around." He runs his beefy hand over the edge of the counter top.

"I don't flirt," I say.

Sal doesn't stop. "But this kid didn't take it that way. She thinks she's hot shit and I guess she thought I was coming on to her. I was being nice. Telling her how nice she looked in her tight dress. With a dress like that I thought she would want compliments. What else? She was flirting back too. Leaning into the desk, writing shit down in her book, and bending all low so I could see them."

I look down at him, relieved. "What did you do?"

"What?" His fingertips are white as he tries to smooth over the rough of edges of the counter he didn't sand down.

"Why do I need to know this, Sal?" I throw the dishcloth in the sink.

His hangdog face and glassy eyes tell me before he does. "So you'll know why I'm around the house a little more now."

"You got fired?" I hug my stomach.

He shakes his head then looks me in the eye. "Fired? No, nah, more like suspended."

I let out a sigh I didn't know I was holding in. "How old was she?"

"I don't know. Young." His attention is focused on the counter again.

"Genny's age?"

"No, Jesus Christ, no." Sal's stare is hard and sure.

"Sal, don't fuck around here. We're adults. If you did something with her, I'm going to need to know, now." I pull out another stool from underneath the counter and lean on it.

"Moníca, I teased." He looks at me. "We tease, that's what we do. Talk a little dirty to each other. She talks dirty to me too. She works in the office, Jesus. She talks like that to everybody."

"So at least she's of age, and it's not illegal." I stand straight.

"No, goddamnit. I didn't do nothing with her or to her. Not a goddamn thing." He slams his fist on the counter. "It was someone else, maybe her stupid boyfriend. She was pissed off at him. I know she was, because when I mentioned her tits she said something like, 'You're all alike.' That's why I'm only suspended."

"Now what do we do?" I sit down and think about Regie and Mike. I am going to stop this madness.

"I gotta go to classes for sexual harassment or some shit. When I asked, 'What about her going?' and told them that she talks about my dick all the time, they told me they could fire me, so I left it."

"How could you be so stupid, Sal?" I let my shoulders slump.

"Her fucking attitude about it makes me want to punch her in the face."

"See that," I point in his face, "talking like that. You can't say that kind of—"

"What! I didn't fucking say that to her." Sal points to himself. "Only my crew. I know the difference. I'm not stupid."

I tilt my head to look at his face. "You tell your crew they have nice tits?"

"No." He runs his fingers along the brown grout. "None of them do."

I can't help but smile. "Shit, Sal, what are we going to do? Are you getting paid while you're suspended?"

"No, but Cheno always needs help at the gravel pit. I can help him landscape. He always needs extra hands, and he pays daily."

"You'll be able to handle the classes, the gravel pit, and your brother?"

"When have I ever not been able to handle work?" He grabs my hand.

"Now." I squeeze back. I have his full attention. "Listen, this probably isn't the best time to tell you."

"So then don't." He lets go of my hand. "The boss asked about you. You believe it?"

"Oh."

"After Davidson told me I was suspended, he said, 'What about your wife, Marissa?'"

I laugh and roll my eyes.

"Told him I got you working at the Lamplighter."

I chuckle, even though I'm supposed to be mad. "I can't believe you told him that! He was probably thinking I clean toilets or something."

"No, Moníca, I see the way he looks at you at those stupid picnics. And I knew he was picturing you, Marissa, with your legs wrapped around one of those poles. He's probably there now."

I throw my hands around his shoulders, grateful. "I'm surprised you've kept your job this long."

He lifts me up and places me on his lap. He is rock hard.

The phone rings and Sal picks it up like he's been waiting for the call. "Yeah. This is Mr. Montoya."

I hug him tight, put my head next to his to try to hear the conversation. He twists the phone toward my ear. I can hear the unaccented English of Mrs. Rodriguez, the principal at Gabe's school.

"We'll be right there," we both say.

Liliana Rodriguez's paneled office is just like her, dull and boring, like she copied everything out of a catalog, down to the shiny gold apple paperweight. She stands when we enter but stays behind her desk like it's her shield. The bright spot in the room is Gabe, but he won't look up. It must be bad.

"Hello, Mr. and Mrs. Montoya." I have to reach over the desk to shake her hand. Sal makes her reach toward him, and now her face is red from the effort. She still looks like the uncomfortable, nervous girl I ignored in these hallways twenty years ago. I sit down in one of the chairs next to Gabe, and Sal stands behind the chair.

"Have a seat, Mr. Montoya." Liliana opens her hand toward the seat on the other side of Gabe.

Sal hesitates, and I think he's going to say something stupid, but he does as he's told. Liliana smiles. She takes a seat too.

"Liliana, what's the problem?" I realize my mistake when she tilts her head and stares sideways like a quail. I remember her nickname in high school, codorniz, Niz for short, and I cough to hide my smile. "Ah, Dr. Rodriguez, can you tell us why you called us in?"

She sits back in her maroon leather chair and folds her arms across her chest. "Why don't we let Gabriel explain?"

Sal and I focus on Gabe, who still won't look up. Sal taps him on the elbow and Gabe looks up at me. I gasp when I see the left side of his face red with what looks like a rash and the beginnings of black eye. "What happened?"

"I told you, Mom." Gabe stares at the apple on Liliana's desk. "I told you he was a bully."

Dr. Rodriguez leans in and ducks her head to catch Gabe's eye. "Who is the bully here?"

Gabe gives her a harsh glare and he looks exactly like his father. The look shocks me, not because I've never seen him use it, but because he is so blatantly trying to intimidate Liliana, in front of us. I start thinking back to our conversation in the kitchen. Could skinny Regie Junior bully anybody? How could I be so stupid? So blind? This can't be my Gabe. Who is he? I look at Sal, who puts his hand on Gabe's shoulder. If he's hiding his girlfriend from me, why wouldn't he hide this? I gave this kid my okay to hurt someone. My blessing to beat him at will.

"You have it wrong," Gabe bunches his hands into fists.

"Watch yourself, Gabriel," I say, low and steady.

His face is back to normal, like a kid's when he looks at me. "It wasn't like that, Mom. Honest. Coach Minor jumped in and stopped it. He did this to me."

"What?" Sal sits up. "Where is this Coach Minor?"

Liliana raises her hand like a crossing guard. "Mr. Montoya, Gabe was very agitated. We have at least twenty witnesses and Gary, Coach Minor, was only trying to calm him down."

"From the looks of my son, I'd say Coach Minor was the one agitated."

" They both fell to the ground and, unfortunately, Gabe hit the floor hard. We thought he was trying to hurt Reginaldo. They have had trouble before."

"I was trying to tell everybody that Junior was hurting himself." Gabe rubs his index finger over his wrist. He looks at me and then Sal. "No one would listen. Junior was inside the bathroom with a knife, one of those big hunting ones. He was cutting himself. Acting out of it, saying, 'This is how they cut his fingers off and this is how they said they'd cut mine.' Junior dropped the knife and I was going to pick it up when Coach Minor ran in. I guess he thought I stabbed him or something because he tackled me."

Liliana clears her throat. "Coach Minor is in the conference room talking to the police right now."

"I was going to stop him. I was." Gabe's eyes tear up, and Sal rubs the back of his neck as I take his hand.

"We're so sorry you had to see that, Gabriel," Liliana says.

"You're going to be, when we get through with this school." I stand and have everyone's attention.

Liliana stands with open arms and says, "We didn't know, Monica, Mrs. Montoya. How were we supposed to know? The two had been fighting before. Gabriel has teased him since the beginning of the school year, we thought—"

"You didn't fucking think, Niz. No one did." Sal takes his arm off Gabe and stands too.

Her small round eyes don't blink, but her mouth quivers as she says, "Mr. Montoya, I understand you're upset, but there is no need to use that kind of language here."

"Fuck that shit, fuck this all." He slams a fist on the desk. Gabe and I jump. "You know us. We grew up together. Stop this. How is the kid?"

"The kid? Oh, Reginaldo will be fine, for now. He's been admitted to Thomason with lacerations and self-inflicted stab wounds. He cut the tip of a finger off."

"Jesus Christ," Sal says. "You tell his father? His mother?"

That's just it, Mr. . . . Sal." Liliana smooths her hand over the apple and looks as if she's about to cry. "Didn't you see the news? Reginaldo's father was found dead last night."

Sal shuts his eyes so tight his face seems to fold into itself, and I blink. I can't stop blinking. I sit down, then try to stand but can't seem to.

"You okay, Mom?" I hear Gabe.

"What happened?" I say.

"I'm not sure, but this morning I heard on the radio that a man was found in a dumpster at the Big 8. And when I got to school, this . . ."

"That can't be right," Sal says.

I know everyone is talking, but I can't hear them. I see Gabe stand up and look at me. All three of them are staring. I think about Regie's face above mine at Red Sands. I can see his black eye. I remember the lizard tattoo on the man's arm. I know it was him. I can identify him, but if I do then Sal will know. Everyone will know. It could have been me. What if they had found us together? What was I doing? What am I doing? How could I be so careless? So reckless? What am I doing? Sal touches my shoulder.

"Mom?" I hear Gabe's voice. "Why is she crying so much, Dad? Make her stop."

I can't stop. It could have been me. It could have been the baby. I touch my stomach and Niz's white-knuckle grip on the golden apple helps me focus. "I'm pregnant."

"Mom, it's okay," Gabe says.

"I'm pregnant," I say again louder.

"What did you say?" Sal's grip tightens.

"Sal, I'm pregnant." I look up and can't stop shaking.

"How many months, Mónica?" He steps toward me. "Why didn't you say anything?"

"I can't breathe." I need to get out of the office. What I need is to see Regie. Call him. I saw him last night. I was with him last night. We were together last night. Was it the man with the tattoo?

Why the dumpster? Did they chop off his fingers? Why the Big 8? What if they saw us? What if they know about me?

"Mom, Mom, say something. You're freaking me out. Dad, what's wrong with her?"

"Your mom's been through a lot this morning, m'ijo. We need to find Genny and get her out of here."

Sal pulls me up from the chair.

"Should I call the nurse?" Liliana points to her desk. "I'll call for Genny."

"I'm really sorry, Mom." Gabe takes my arm and leads me out.

"No, no, she'll be fine. We'll finish this another time." Sal points to the floor and then to Gabe.

"Yes, another time. Tomorrow, no, not tomorrow, it's assembly. Day after. Gabe needs to give his statement. He needs to talk to the police too."

"Liliana, we need to go." Sal is holding me up and walking out the door. "They can come to the house."

I see Genny run to the car. "Did you hear what happened? Junior's dad killed himself. They found him in the dumpster at the Big 8."

All three of us say, "Shut up." For the first time ever, Genny does. Once I'm in the car, I relax. No one talks and I look out the window as we pass the Big 8, the yellow tape around the green dumpster, and I think of Regie in there. Did they dump him feet first? Did he suffer? Did they torture him? I sob out loud, thinking of him lying in the trash, struggling in the filth, him yelling and no one there to hear him. I want to scream but I can't. So I sit with my eyes closed and imagine myself in the ocean. Floating down until I feel the sandy bottom and push off with my toes. It's not a good push. Weak. I use my arms to help me go up. Slow. It is slow, too slow. It's taking forever. I'm running out of air and I cry.

"I'm sorry, Mom." Gabe pats my shoulder.

"She'll be fine, Gabe. She will. There's a lot going on. Hormones too."

"Dad, what's going on?" Genny says.

"M'ija, your mom is pregnant." He smiles wide.

"I knew it. I knew it. Who eats chili dogs? I knew it. I knew it."

"Shhh, now. We'll talk more when we get home," Sal says.

I'm grateful. With my eyes closed and the movements of the car, I can feel waves on my face, the wave of someone's kick. I feel the waves and keep swimming up until I don't feel anything.

When I open my eyes it's quiet, dark, and I am in my own bed. I rub my stomach, close my eyes, and picture Regie.

There is knock on the bedroom door. "Moníca, you up?"

"Yeah."

Sal walks in with a plate. "I've got some 7UP and crackers here." As he sets everything on the nightstand next to the bed his brow furrows. He sits down. "You don't have to worry. It will be okay. I'm going to talk to Mr. Davidson tomorrow. I'll explain the situation, apologize to everyone, and be back at work by the end of the week."

I sob and roll away from him.

"You look like you could use a drink." I hear the hiss of the soda can opening and loud steps in the hallway.

"I got here as fast as I could. Is the baby okay?" Bernie looks from me to Sal and then back to me. "Moníca, Moníca, I'm so sorry. So sorry."

"This is why you stayed at Bernie's the other night?" Sal stands. I'm quiet.

She points to me, then to the air, and lets herself fall onto the bed next to me. "We talk."

"Yes, I needed someone to talk to." I roll toward her and touch her arm in warning. Her mouth opens then closes. I focus my attention on Sal. "I'm sorry. I should have talked to you first. I was planning to tell you. When the time was right."

Sal wipes his face with a hand. "I haven't been easy to talk to, Moníca. I should have known when you said you were on that stupid diet." He smiles and I know it's okay.

"I'm kinda hungry. Would you make me something real to eat?"

"You should be. It's almost midnight." He looks relieved, ready to do something.

"You fed the kids?" I look up at him.

"Who else was gonna do it? My wife was passed out in bed. I'm answering a lot of questions from Genny, but I won't let her in here until you tell me to."

"Thanks. Potatoes and baloney sounds good to me."

"It's your lucky day. I just need to heat them up." He walks out of the room.

I sit up in bed and raise my voice. "Sal."

From the hallway he says, "Yeah?"

"Thank you."

"Don't thank me until after you taste the papas." I hear his steps in the hall.

Bernie is wide-eyed on the edge of the bed. We stay this way until we hear kitchen noises.

Bernie clucks her tongue and whispers absently, "Hasta la vista, bizca. Hasta la vista, bizca. Hasta la vista, bizca."

We're so quiet that we can hear the hum of the microwave oven coming from the kitchen. Bernie grabs one of the pillows on the bed.

I let myself fall back. "I can't see a cross-eyed person without laughing. You know it's not good to laugh when you look at a cross-eyed person."

Bernie smiles, then nods.

I giggle. "Right here." I point to my forehead and Bernie looks at me. "He always put his fist on my forehead. He did it to keep me from clinging to him as he slipped out of the car!"

"Yes." She punches the yellow pillow she is holding.

"I'd cross my eyes at him through my tears." I hold back tears. "And no matter how mad I was at him, when he said it, 'Hasta la vista, bizca,' I would smile."

"He told us the same thing."

"I did smile, every time." I look up and slap at the pillow in Bernie's arms. "I loved his smile, like an upside-down half-moon in a scarred sky. I'd like to see that again, or even his back."

"I always thought he had the face of a guarache."

"What? Shoes?"

"No, guarache. His face was bumpy, all the scars from the pimples. Plus, it was shaped like a duck."

"A guarache, yeah, I can see it." I hear the ding of the microwave. Gabe and Sal are talking. "Tell me: Why? Why did we put up with it? Why?"

She shakes her head and squeezes the pillow tighter. She lets out a breath and tries to find the answer in the brown carpet at her feet. "I don't know. It's just the way it was."

I pound my chest and in my deepest voice say, "Mi amor, thees is where I belong, donde estoy acomodo, where I can be me."

She grabs a Kleenex out of her breast pocket, waves it in the air, and chokes up. I can't tell if it's from laughter or tears. "Shut up, ya, you're being disrespectful. He always said that. Always."

"You are my vida. You are where my true life starts and where my real love lives." I choke up and want to sink my teeth into my forearms like I would when Vicente was telling Mom this. "I wanted to *not* hug him, but I did. I always did. I would always think 'What if he doesn't come back?' This will be the last time."

Bernie blots the tears on her face. "Don't tell me no moro. Every time you tell me that I feel . . ." She pats the pillow near her chest.

I look up at the ceiling as Gabe walks in.

"Hi, tía. Um, Mom, I got your food here." He looks nervously around.

"This looks good, m'ijo." Bernie throws the pillow behind her as she gets up. It lands on my face. "I'll take it. You and your dad did a good job."

"You want a plate too?"

"No, I already ate. It's too late to be eating. Thanks, m'ijo." She holds the plate in one hand and reaches for the bedroom door with the other.

Gabe leaves.

"You are the luckiest person I know." She picks at the plate as she walks toward me.

"Regie is dead." I look at her.

"What?" She sets the plate of food on the nightstand.

"They killed him."

She claps her hands together. "See what I mean."

I throw the pillow at her as hard I can and it hits her legs softly and falls to the floor. "No, I don't. He's dead, Bernie. A man is dead. "

"I'm sorry, Moníca. I'm sorry. For him not so much, but for his family, yes." She bends to pick it up.

"We lose all the men in our life." I realize that I don't feel sad, and I wonder why. I think of my father. "I guess Vicente was preparing me."

We are quiet together until I say, "I watched Vicente get lost at the turnstiles. I would try to point him out to Mom when I spotted him again on the bridge. She never looked. I watched him until he disappeared behind the cement hill that led to you. So why?"

"Stop asking." She pretends to throw the pillow and I raise my arms, ready. "What do you want, Moníca? ¿Qué? You want me to shit out a father for you? One that comes home after work and pats your head, tells you he loves you, eats food at the table? Who lives like that? No one, and if they tell they do, son mentirosos. Life is not simple, easy. It's a struggle every day. People were meant to struggle and I, we, just the same, not different, not special."

"Why'd I let him do this to me? Why would he give me this life? Why?" I stare at the pillow in her arms.

"Your life? What about mine?" She stands up, and I flinch, waiting for the pillow. "I wanted to be a nurse, but then he left for good. Working took all my time. When I got here I looked you up, beautiful and carefree. You with your mother's fair face, living with opportunities thrown at you."

"I was talking about Regie. But it's her fault." I point at her as she paces. "From the first time your mother let him cross that bridge. Why?"

"Dumb, simple, like me blaming Josie. You're asking the wrong question." She sways near the door.

"What's the right one?" Both my hands are in the air.

She puts one hand on her hip and points south with the other. "Why did he marry?"

I wave a finger at her. "No, why did you put up with him?" I point at her like I'm ringing a doorbell. "He told her about us."

She puts her hand to her chest and drops her chin onto it. "He loved me and he loved you too."

"How many others you think he loved?" I point to the same spot she did earlier.

Her eyes tear up. "You watch it. ¿Entiendes? He may be dead, but I'm still alive."

When I look into her eyes, I want to cry and slap her at the same time. She is protecting him and me too. I back off.

"Mom always stopped talking, crying even, when we got off the freeway. Like clockwork." I stand up, ready for anything.

"Ya, shut up, will you? I can't hear no more." She waves her hand, then wipes her tears away. The hazel electric eyes Vicente gave her are dull, and she looks more like him than ever.

"I'm just trying to figure out why we're so stupid." I begin to pace. "What the hell is wrong with us?"

"Nothing." Bernie shrugs her shoulders.

"Oh, so this is normal? Sharing a father is normal? You get him weekends and we get him weekdays is normal?" I stand facing away from her.

"Normal? ¿Normal? ¿Que es normal? You want me to forget the fifteen years he came home every week. Era mal but he was also good. You want me to hate him? It is not something I can just forget, asi." She snaps her fingers. "Like nothing. I'm not that American, yet."

I don't see her but I hear the snap and I sit down so that the springs creak. "I'd figure I'd be all cried out by now as many times as we drove him over to her."

"To her. To her?" She points her finger up. "Watch your mouth. You drove him to the bridge back to his family. ¿Entiendes?" She grabs my arm and I pull away from her grip and scoot to the edge of the bed, as far away from her nails as I can get without seeming afraid.

I laugh. "Yeah, we did, didn't we?" I shake my head. "It took us an hour to get there."

"It takes me fifteen minutes to get to the bridge from . . ." Bernie smiles and nods her head.

"Drive friendly, my butt. Everyone was always flipping us off." I smile and scoot toward the middle of the bed. "Going forty on the freeway doesn't make you many friends."

She paces. "Your mother probably had a lot to say to him, before—"

"We were pathetic." I wrinkle my nose, thinking about Mom packing Vicente's suitcase so he could go back. When his real family got to be too much for him he'd cross over, and when we got to be too much he'd cross back. I never got used it, never.

Bernie gets her face so close to mine that I can smell the ginger on her breath from the marranito she ate earlier. "You weren't pathetic. We weren't. We loved him."

Instead of looking away, I get up and step toward her. "I just want to know. Why did they let him? Why would they do this to themselves? To us?" I have goose bumps on my arms and am ready to flee.

"Porqué lo quisieron," Bernie whispers without looking up.

I walk toward her.

"What exactly did they love about him? His not coming home, taking their youth? What was it? Why, why did they stay?"

She looks at me, and her eyes squint. "Lo quisieron, lo quisieron . . ."

Bernie's voice, "lo quisieron," fills me for a second, fills me the way taking the rigid leaves from the agave in my hands does. The way bending the tentacle back until I hear it pop satisfies me. "And that's an explanation? They loved him. You know Josie sprayed her perfume on his underwear after she washed it."

Bernie nods her head. "Chanel Number Five. She even put her underwear in the bag."

"Really?"

"I'm the one that opened it. I kept them, and when Graciela found them she would use them. He stayed with us even when Graciela came along."

"He was a saint." I roll my eyes.

"No, not at all." She shakes her head. "He didn't want mamí to be shamed."

"Everyone here knew he was married on the other side. Josie knew it and still they had me. Everyone knew, and they wouldn't ever let me forget, especially the men. They'd promise a house on the West Side for me and Mom if I would just let them take me for a ride, take me to a party, drive me to Juárez, and if I didn't tell Vicente. They said I was beautiful like my mother. Some said I was better looking, especially at twelve when my chichis were just starting to show traces of the woman I am now. They'd grab at them. I would laugh, excited by their attention, and then walk home rubbing myself because of the soreness."

Bernie wraps her arms around me and I let her. I cry into her shoulder. She cries too.

"I loved him too," I cry out, and I don't know if my tears are for Regie, Vicente, or me.

"You think your mother will like me?" I stare up at her hazel eyes.

"They're going to love you. You act exactly like Vicente. It's like having him here, only better, because you're a woman."

CHAPTER TEN

Rest in Peace

SAL WIPES THE sweat from his temples with his thumb before he opens the car door. When I open the passenger side, the heat rushes over me like warm water and it feels like I am drowning. When I sit, I twist the air conditioner knobs.

"Ouch, ouch, will you hurry up and start the car?" I twist the black plastic, then blow on my fingers.

"Stop it, goddamnit, you're going to ruin the car." Sweat drips from Sal's head onto his navy trousers. He drapes his suit coat across the back seat.

"I can't make it worse than it already is." I give up on the knobs. "Just go, will you, and let's get this over with."

The midafternoon sun makes everything look white. We drive in silence, past the beige sand dotted with tufts of green weeds. The weeds sprouting out of the dryness make me think of when Regie had a goatee, and I sigh. Facial hair I'll never get to stroke again. We pass the tall yuccas that remind me of the characters in those Japanese comics Gabe always has his face in. The neon-colored billboards advertise beer and telephone service. I feel Salvador's gaze on me and shift in my seat so that he can't see my face. Gas stations, fast-food restaurants, Mexican-food cafes, and strip malls are a blur. Rental houses, pool halls, bars, strip joints, and liquor stores. I remember the bars and liquor stores Regie and I have walked in as they whiz by. I look up at the aqua-blue sky to keep from crying.

"You feeling okay?" Sal whispers.

"Just a little sick." I hug my stomach and stare out the window. "I'm glad Gabe didn't want to come."

"I think it was a mistake." Sal shakes his head. "We should have made him. Later, when he's older, he's going to be sorry."

"I don't think so. It's better to bury the bad and forget it."

"I can't believe autopsies take so long." Sal taps the steering wheel.

"It must have killed Sandra not to be able to bury Regie right away," I choke.

"You okay?" Sal caresses my stomach. "You don't sound right."

I nod. The stringy clouds remind me of webs, traps set by black widows in the corners of the garage. It was a trap. A trap that Regie got caught up in. He was too stupid to deal, too stupid. If he hadn't called it all off, if he'd been with me instead of . . . who? He was just a kid, like a kid playing in the traffic on I-10. Out the window nothing moves but the cars on the gummy tar road. When I squint and look out of the windshield the black asphalt sparkles, the cement sidewalks glow, and the gray rock fences seem to disappear in the glitter of the heat. There is beauty everywhere.

"You know where it is, right?" I turn and stare at Sal. He looks uncomfortable with his shirt buttoned to the neck.

He cringes but keeps his eyes on the road. "Yes, of course I do. I've been to plenty of funerals there."

"Don't pass it like you always do." I can't help myself. His simple life makes me angry and I want him to suffer too.

"When the hell have we ever been here together for me to pass it up?" Sal hits the steering wheel with his hand.

"I meant like you miss the turn whenever we go anywhere." I turn on the radio.

He loosens his grip on the wheel, steers with his thumb and pointing finger near his legs, and grinds his teeth.

"It's right here, right here. This is it, Sal." I don't want to miss the service.

"I know, I know," he says, trying to keep his voice steady.

Sal circles around the mortuary to find a parking space. We walk a block and now Salvador has sweat rings under his arms and I can feel the wetness on the small of my back. When we walk inside the air-conditioned room, Sal lets out a sigh and I inhale the too-sweet smell of flowers. Inside the chapel the priest has started, and most of the thirty people in attendance sit in the back pews, except for family. As we walk down the aisle, the men and women bend their heads toward one another to whisper. I start to sweat again. I feel faint when I see the black casket at the front of the church. I drop myself into an empty seat nearest me. Salvador keeps walking until a woman across the aisle tugs at his shirt sleeve. She moves over a few inches and pats the seat next to her and smiles. He nods his head and sits. Sal looks behind him and over at me. I nod, then stare straight ahead to watch Arturo, Regie's brother who was at the podium when we walked in.

"My brother could fix anything. Todos aqui have had something fixed by Regie, a car, radio, toaster, que no? One lady, one time brought him a cat to fix," Arturo says, his voice breaking. The crowd laughs and he says, "No shit. Oh, sorry, padre. He told her, 'No, señora; I don't do that kind of fixing. You need to take him to the vet.' She said the vet charged too much and how much would he charge to try? He knocked his knuckles against his Camaro and looked at the floor for a long time. I got scared because, híjole, I thought the crazy f—, um, he was gonna do it, but then he said, 'No, señora. No puedo. It wouldn't be right.' Yeah, my brother, he could fix anything, except . . ."

Father Solano interrupts, "Arturo, gracias, gracias for those wonderful words about Renaldo."

I see Sal shake his head at the preacher's mistake. I sit up straight in the pew, grateful Sal isn't next to me because he'd be asking about the baby. He'd probably be able to feel me trembling. I want to cry out. I am sweating from the effort it takes to hold back my tears. I look at my hands and flex my fingers. Regie reminded me so much of Vicente. Not so much the way he looked but how he made me feel—happy and alive. I shake my head, thinking about how it would have been living on the other side with Bernie and his real family. They're both dead. Maybe I'd be dead too.

"Yes, yes, he was a saint," says Arturo, ignoring the priest and continuing. "Even if you don't believe it. He'd help anyone, and he loved life."

I look up from my hands and see that Arturo is staring right at me, repeating that Regie was a God-fearing man. Then I realize that I am shaking my head from side to side and I stop. I look at the back of Sal's head and can see he is fanning himself. I gaze at my heels. Sweat trickles from my hairline down the side of my cheek. I fix my eyes on the wide back of Regie's pregnant wife, Sandra, in the front pew.

"My brother was a vago, yes." Arturo leans into the podium. "He was funny. When he got sent to prison the first time, it was because he was caught sneaking into a Snoopy's bar. He went in through the vent system. He told me, 'The jura came just as I was pouring my first jara.' And when they asked him how he got in, he told them that he was leaning against the back door and it just opened and he fell inside."

I smile and many people laugh. I make fists of my hands and am grateful when Father Solano takes the microphone from Arturo, who wanted to sing Regie's favorite song. The man never could hold his liquor and I worry that they talked about me.

After the incantations, Sal and I meet in the middle of the aisle like we're getting married. He holds his arm out for me to take. I am grateful. He insisted we come and support someone from the neighborhood. I'm glad I came. As we wait in line to give our condolences to Regie's family, Sal puts his arm around me.

"You feeling okay?"

"I'm fine. Fine. I just want to saludar and get out of here."

"We will."

The first person in line is Arturo, and he has tears streaming down his cheeks. When he sees Sal, he falls into his embrace.

Sal holds him up and takes him by the neck. "Be strong, ese, be strong."

This is enough to make Arturo stand tall and wipe his face. "Thanks. Thanks for coming."

Sal passes him and is hugging Regie's wife. When Arturo sees me, his eyes open wide. He looks at Sal's back and then at me and my stomach. He knows, and before he can open his mouth I give him a hard hug. I whisper in his ear, "This isn't his. I had a test."

"Pero." He holds me at arm's length.

"They can tell nowadays. It's not." I give him a stern look.

He looks relieved and sighs. "I'm going to miss him."

"So am I. So am I."

"Thanks for coming."

Regie's wife, Sandra, turns to talk with a woman behind her when I try to offer her my condolences. I wait for her to finish, but after what seems like a minute of seeing her back Sal takes my arm and leads me toward the coffin. I am dazed. I thought no one knew about us. I wonder if Sal will find out. I hesitate at first and I want to talk to Sandra, but Sal's gentle tugs lead me to where Regie's mother is weeping. When she sees us, she ignores me and takes hold of Salvador. From over the head of Mrs. Juarez, he takes my hand and pulls me toward him so that I take a step back.

"We knew Regie from the old neighborhood and we are so sorry to see him go." My words come in a rush.

"I'm going to miss my little boy," she says, looking at Sal. "He was a good boy and I believe he will meet me up in heaven. We had to have closed casket because . . ."

She starts to cry and allows me to embrace her as Sal gives her a hug too. As I let her go, the man next in line behind me embraces her. Sal gives me his arm and I take his elbow, and we walk down the aisle toward the exit. I feel ashamed. Outside in the too-bright sun, I give his arm a squeeze before he opens the car door for me and I step inside. He walks to the driver's side and opens his door. He starts the car and I fiddle with the air knobs.

Temples dripping, Sal says, "Stop it, goddamnit. You're going to ruin my car."

I stop fiddling. Sal puts the car in drive and nudges the car into the funeral procession line.

"Regie Junior wasn't there," I say.

"I don't think the kid's in good shape."

We drive down Montana Boulevard, passing sand and tumble-weeds, strip joints, fast-food restaurants, motels, strip malls, pool halls, auto-parts stores, mechanics shops, junkyards, and the mountains.

"This isn't the way to the cemetery," I say.

"Yes, it is."

"No, it's not, because Regie's going to be buried at Evergreen and Evergreen is on Alameda."

"No, Evergreen is on Montana. Sunset is on Alameda."

"No, it's not."

"Damn it, Monica. You're wrong. Evergreen is on Montana. I think these people know where they're going." He points to the procession in front of him.

"I'm telling you, it's not. We buried my mom there, and soon we're going to bury Dad. This is not it. We're all going to look really stupid going to the wrong cemetery."

"Monica, this is the way. I pass it every day on my way to work."

"No, it's not."

"Yes, it is." He slams his fists against the steering wheel.

"Sal, this isn't the right way, damn it." I am sure.

Sal swerves into the large parking lot of a discount strip mall. My head grazes the passenger side window from the force of the turn.

He says, "You think you know so much? You're always right? You're acting crazy. You've been crazy since the baby. You gotta stop this. You'll hurt her. Yourself. Do you hear me, Monica?"

"I just know that that isn't the way." I point west toward the purple Franklins.

Sal looks past me out my window and his scowl turns into a grin.

I raise my eyebrows and look out my window. I giggle, then begin to laugh. The cars in the funeral procession behind us have followed us into the strip mall. They drive every which way like ants whose home has just be disturbed. Sal takes my hand and he laughs with me.

"What makes you think we're having a girl?" I squeeze his hand.

CHAPTER ELEVEN

Bernie's Fortune

FROM MY LIVING room window I see Bernie open the door before she puts the Plymouth in park. She moves quick, like everyone in El Paso who doesn't want their upper lip to bead with sweat. I can't help but smile when she punches the air to the beat of the ranchera music she hears or how easily she steps over the holes and cracks in the asphalt coming toward the house. She doesn't look like she's coming for a funeral service. She looks like she's going to a club. She pats the wetness off of her lip with a yellow tissue, pulls at the hem of her sequined top, and walks toward the back. I can use her help. I need to talk to her about Regie. I've been on the verge of crying all morning. I think this whole service is a big mistake. It was a bad idea to have her family here. But I guess things have to change. Things have changed. I'm just glad she got here before Graciela and her mother. I wonder if I bought enough beer. Gabe did a good job raking the sand near the porch; it looks like brown corrugated steel. I hate to see it messed up. The brinca-brinca is still sagging, but at least Sal put it in the shade and the kids are playing in it. I can hear them laughing. These are all Bernie's people, Vicente's friends and family. These Mexicanos in their stiff cowboy hats, starched shirts, and Levis are so polite. They remind me of birds perched on the cement-and-rock walls surrounding our yard. Too many of the white-and-green plastic chairs are empty, probably uncomfortable. I should have rented chairs, but I gotta admit Sal's wooden spool tables don't look so bad. What am I going to do with seven spools after this?

"Ah, Moníca, am I late?" Bernie hugs me. "You doing okay?"

"Yes, yes, payasa, you're always late." I squeeze her so hard she gasps for air. "Everybody's already here. Almost everybody. Gabriela is bringing Mrs. Gomez, uh, your mom. Does she know where my house is? She knows she's coming to my house? She knows I'm hosting the party?"

"No te preocupes. You worry for nothing. My mom is okay. You'll love her."

"I know I'll love her, will she . . ."

"She's gonna love you like I do, de veras." She looks in my eyes. "You need a beer. Oh, no, never mind, I need one. You look pretty in that dress. You barely show."

I smooth my hand over the small bulge of my stomach. "Oh, come on, I'll show you. Sal's brother Cheno is our bartender. Wasn't my idea. Sal's working for him now. Well, I shouldn't say any more. Just come."

"I remember him. He looks like Sal, no?" Bernie burrows her hand into her cleavage and rearranges the flesh inside her C-cup orange satin bra.

"You be careful with him. He's, he's, ah—how do I say?—Different." I lead her by the hand to the corner of the yard where Cheno stands in the middle of four metal trash cans handing out clear plastic cups filled with beer. I see Bernie comb her hair with her fingers, self-conscious, and I look at Cheno.

"Níca, que onda, gorda?" He holds his arms open.

I touch my belly, then look at his beer belly and try not to cringe.

"You need a jara?" He lifts up a pitcher of beer that sits full on top of a keg and smiles so wide his golden-covered molars show.

Eyes down, Bernie laughs and slaps at my arm.

"Yes, yes, or two cups for me and my sister, Bernie," I say, to introduce the two.

"This is your sister? Why haven't I met her before?" He looks from me to her and back again. He zeroes in on the gold bracelet

Bernie wears and puffs his chest out. "I know who got all the looks in the family."

Bernie giggles like a kid, and I want to slap him.

"All right then, copitas it is. " He sets the pitcher down and jacks the pump four times, tips the plastic cup, and fills it to the brim. A bit splashes out as he hands her a cup. He is drunk. Had he been sober he'd have cussed the waste.

"So whose birthday party is this, Níca?" He nods at me and hands me a cup. "No one tells me nothing."

Bernie gulps her drink and leaves it half-empty. "It's a funeral, our father's."

"Your father?" He points at her with the pump hose in his hand and splashes beer. "So you're sisters?"

"Yes, we told you already." I'm annoyed, and he is enjoying every minute of it.

Bernie pats my arm like I'm a kid. "Me and Moníca share the same father but not the same mother, and Graciela has a different father than me but the same mother." Bernie sways playfully.

"Graciela? Who's that? How the hell you keep track of everybody? I guess it don't matter." He raises his cup to the sky, and as Bernie meets his toast, a young, thin, blonde woman in a miniskirt cuddles in next to him.

"To family, gorda. To family, ah, what was your name again?"

"Bernadette. Bernadette Gomez." Bernie touches her plastic cup to his and nods at the young woman.

He wraps his toasting arm around the woman and we sip our beers. "Family is all we got."

Bernie looks at the younger woman in front of her, and I can tell she's mad by her tight smile. I want to pull her away from here, but she's not going anywhere. I know that hungry look.

"Hi, Cory. You just get here? Did your mother bring you?" I look down at the chipped red polish on Cory's toenails and slowly up to her bleached-blonde hair, trying to make her feel uncomfortable. It makes me feel good to see Bernie grin at my efforts. They can't be together, these two. It would be a disaster—Cheno and Bernie. "How is she?"

"Fine." Cory frowns and slips a ring-studded hand around Cheno's waist and squeezes.

"M'ija, hold up, yeah? My panza is still sore from my fall." Cheno pulls away from her.

"Oye, sorry, I forget." She lets go of his waist and gently slugs his shoulder. "And don't call me m'ija."

"What?" Cheno laughs and pulls at the woman's shaggy hair. "M'ija? You're my hijita, my fine little girl. Everybody says it." He pulls on her hair harder and makes kissing noises. She laughs and pulls the clump of her hair out of his hands.

"Qué te pasó?" Bernie says, snapping away Cheno's attention.

He squints at her and his eyes linger on her cleavage. "I fell at a jobsite. I do these side jobs when my business is slow. I was hungover, moving Sheetrock with Tony. I stepped in a hole and busted my ass and the Sheetrock. Fucking foreman took it out of my pay. It's just my luck."

"You gotta be more careful," I say. "You're getting older and can't be doing the same things you were doing at twenty."

"I'm still doing the same things, qué no?" He squeezes Cory tight.

She giggles, places her hands on his potbellied stomach, and her fingers find an opening inside his shirt. "Oh, sí, hurt y todo."

"What's your business?" Bernie leans in toward Cheno to give him a better look at her cleavage.

"Landscaping. They say I'm an artist."

"Well, we better go find Sal." I take Bernie's arm before I have to say something nice about him. "Say hello to your mother, Cory, when she takes you home. You are still living with her, no?"

Cory frowns and nods at me.

Cheno laughs out loud at my comment and Bernie smiles wide when our backs are turned. I am worried. We walk through the crowd and stop for Bernie to give hugs and introduce me to her family along the way.

"Did you see his forearms?" Bernie says to herself.

"They're big because he's spent time in jail. El bote, Bernie. ¿Me entiendes?" I stop and pull on her arm. "He's not—"

"I'd like to feel them around me just once. That full head of hair. Men his age don't have that much hair. It's beautiful."

Bernie's thoughts are somewhere else. She's in a stupor and I can't help but laugh. I know the feeling. Knew it. I frown. "It's your life. Just watch your wallet. I'm not kidding around."

"Does he like young women?" She bounces to the trumpets blasting from the speakers set on the windowsills.

"He likes women with money." I step onto the cement patio. "That's the truth."

She kicks sand out of her open-toed pumps and smiles so wide that even I want her to have Cheno. "Let's go find Sal. I have a lot of questions for him."

"How about you help me in the kitchen with the food? At least tell me if your mom and sister will like—"

"Ay, you worry too much. Everything is already perfect. They are going to love it, love you, Genny, Gabe, and Sal."

We walk through conversations and children run past us as we enter the house through the sliding back door. Inside, doo-wop music plays and mixes with the ranchera that Gabe blasts outside. Smaller groups of men and women talk in hushed voices on my couches and recliners. Sal is nowhere in sight, and Bernie sighs.

"Okay, I'll check out the food." She points her fingers like a gun toward the kitchen.

"I bought all the carne from Barron's. It's the best meat in town."

She sticks her fingers in her ears and nods. I lean in. "You think this will be enough?"

She glances at the four aluminum trays lined on the counter top filled with chicken, beef, and pork. "Yes, yes. Where is Sal?"

"Come on, damn it." I march out of out of the kitchen and she's right next to me. I am not surprised to see Cheno crouched next to a coffee table in front of a middle-aged man wearing black-framed glasses, who is seated on my plush couch. Bernie scans the room, looking for Cory, and then walks toward Cheno. Cheno winks at Bernie. The man stands up and hugs her, then sits back down and shakes his head.

"Turner," Bernie says, "this is my sister, Mónica."

"Hi, Mónica." Turner stands up and hugs me. "I thought Graciela was your sister?"

"She's my sister too. We just don't have the same mother." Bernie speaks loud.

He ignores her. I'm not sure if he heard her. "My mother doesn't like for me to drink. Oh, no, not at all. She would kill me if I ever thought about drinking." Turner slips a finger under the white elastic band attached to his glasses and scratches his scalp.

"Nah, man, your mother would be okay with it." Cheno pours beer into a cup from the pitcher on the table, then sets it down. "She would want you to have good time."

"No, she doesn't want me to drink." Turner gazes at the empty space between Cheno and Bernie. "She's watching."

"Where? Where is she?" Cheno says, holding the cup.

"Right there, here next to Aunt Bernie." Turner winces because the band slaps his head when he moves his finger to point at the air.

"He's your nephew." I look at her.

"No, my mother's. It's just easier for him if he calls us all tía." Bernie looks to her right.

"No, on the other side," Turner says.

Bernie looks at Cheno and puts her arm in the air as if she were hugging someone by the neck. "Before your mom died, Turner, she asked me to look after you." Bernie turns and stares at the air she is hugging. "Ofelia, would it be okay if Turner drank a beer?"

Cheno pops up from the floor and looks from Turner to the air and back. "You see, Turner? She says it's okay. It's okay."

He picks up the cup filled with beer and hands it to Turner, who takes it and scratches the back of his head under the elastic, then looks from Bernie to his invisible mother. "Okay, if Mom says it's all right then I'll have just one." He takes one gulp and nearly finishes the cup.

Bernie whispers to Cheno, "I have to talk to you."

He nods his head and picks up the pitcher to pour Turner another. I am speechless. Bernie is acting insane, completely insane. Everything is wrong. I can't think straight. I'm sick to my stomach. I don't know why I agreed to do this. I need air. I need to see Regie. Genny walks by and I grab her arm.

"Mom, let go. I gotta watch for Aunt Graciela and her mother. I'm the lookout, remember?"

As she walks away toward the kitchen, I yell, "She's not your aunt."

I see Cheno and Bernie whispering into each other's ears, and Bernie is smiling like she won a prize and nodding her head. Gabe is in the kitchen guarding his stereo, cassette tapes, and albums, and I am alone in a house filled with people. Where is Sal? I step onto the linoleum floor and stick my fingers in my ears because the music is so loud. I see Gabe using exaggerated hand gestures to communicate with Genny. He is pointing out the window, and she turns around. We all watch from the window as a burgundy-haired Señora Gomez shuffles into the backyard with a walker and Graciela with the identical hair color walks in behind her. The frail-looking woman stops, clutches her chest, and smiles. She composes herself and turns to her daughter, her mouth formed in an O, and tears stream down her sagging, liver-spotted cheeks. I turn to look for Bernie and see her walking out the sliding glass doors that lead into the backyard.

Gabe lowers the volume of the music outside, and I want him to turn it off so we can hear them talk. Gabe, Genny, and I see Bernie hug Graciela, then we lose sight of them both as men, women, and children surround them.

"Who brought her?" Gabe asks.

"I think that's Aunt Graciela, Bernie's sister." Genny puts her hand on Gabe's shoulders.

Before I can say, *She's not your aunt,* Genny says, "I mean Gracey."

"So this is what we've been waiting for?"

I jump at the sound of Sal's voice. "Where the hell have you been?" I say louder than I wanted, still watching the crowd.

"You okay?" He rubs my shoulders and puts his arms around me. "You look beautiful enough to have my baby."

105

My skin tingles and I lean into Sal. "Well, we gonna stay in here all day, or are wo gonna meet Bernie's family?"

Genny takes my hand, and Gabe pushes a cassette tape into the tape deck. Genny leads me outside onto the porch, and I walk along to Juan Gabriel crooning "Amor Eterno . . ." I sing along and wipe the corners of my eyes.

I rub my hands together, nervous about meeting my father's real wife. I stand behind Bernie, who is talking to several of her cousins at once, and wait for my introduction. When the group of people walk away, another wave of cousins comes and I am ignored again. Señora Gomez and Graciela are now seated like security guards near the makeshift table within sight of Cheno. They are talking to each other intensely, and Bernie is flirty and animated like I've never seen her. Graciela and her mother don't notice me at all. Señora Gomez looks angry.

In a loud voice Graciela says to her mother, "I would choose Bonnie Blanco." Then she looks over at Bernie. "I like your top. Is it the same one from my wedding?"

"Yes." Bernie pulls at the hem and dusts off invisible lint from her breast.

"It still fits? Wow," Graciela says.

"Just barely." Bernie stands and I notice that Cheno is watching her. "Choose Bonnie for what?" she says in a high voice I've never heard her use before.

Graciela points to her mother and then back at herself. "Ay, Mom. We go to water aerobics together. We play volleyball in the water and she, all the time, wants me to pick her to be on my team. She doesn't want to be picked last."

I am surprised that they exercise. I forget that they've been in the States for at least five years now.

Señora Gomez sighs and nods. "Who would you pick—me or Bonnie Blanco?"

"To play?" Bernie says. "It depends."

"Depends?" Señora's painted-on eyebrows wrinkle.

"Yeah." Bernie tugs her top out of her folds. "Are we playing for fun or to win?"

Graciela leans forward, reaches for her comb in her back pocket, then runs it through her hair. "Pues, to win, what else?"

"Well, then I would pick Bonnie." Bernie looks at Graciela combing her hair.

"What?" Her mother's mouth opens.

"I would—"

"I heard what you said. I'm not sorda, yet. I just can't believe it. You'd pick a total stranger over me?" Señora Gomez grunts as she struggles out of her chair to stand.

Bernie touches her shoulder. "She's not a total stranger. I went to prepa with her."

Graciela laughs as she puts the comb back in her pocket.

"You know what I mean." Señora Gomez shakes her head.

"Mom, you can barely walk, and I've seen you play, you're afraid of the ball. You think people win because they're lucky or something?" Bernie steps back.

"That's not the point!" Her mother grinds her walker into the cement patio.

"Yeah, it is the point. You make your own luck by choosing right." Bernie watches as Cheno storms away from Cory, who is next to the kegs surrounded by several men.

"Agringada, that's how you sound. Congratulations. You're American. You don't need no papers. You're already selfish and forgetful of your family." Señora Gomez takes a step and grips her walker.

Graciela's face is red and fat tears roll down her cheeks as she laughs silently. "Te dije. You just don't want to hear the truth."

Señora Gomez stops in front of me. "And you? Who the hell are you? Who would you pick? Someone who could help you win or your own blood?"

"I uh . . . uh . . . I'm Mónica Montoya, señora. Welcome to my house. I'm so pleased you are here."

There is a second of recognition and surprise in her eyes. In a swift scan of the eyes she looks me up and then down. She raises her walker off of the floor. "Who, damn it? Who would you choose?"

I know that this moment is somehow important. That I'll never forget this because Graciela is no longer laughing, Bernie has stopped searching the crowd for Cheno and is looking at us too, and this woman is waiting for my answer.

"If we were playing for fun?" I say, and I wipe my nose with the back of my hand, nervous. "If we were playing for fun? You'd be the first person I picked."

"Coming from you, a gabacha, it's an answer I would expect. Vicente liked gabachos and how they don't care about family. He said he could breathe better aqui. He thought like a gabacho. Most men would have left after Gracey. He would find this all funny, but me, no." Señora Gomez hobbles off toward the house. "Me, I can barely breathe here. You got anything to eat around here?"

Genny touches Señora Gomez's arm. "Hello, Señora Gomez. I'm Genny Montoya, Monica's daughter. Let me show you what we have."

I watch them walk away. Graciela steps in front of me and points to my face. "You're coldhearted. You must be family." She hunches over like her mother and points a finger at me. "You think this is funny?"

She laughs, and finally I do too. I let out the breath I didn't know I was holding in, nod, and laugh as she puts her arms around me and hugs me. She smells and feels like Bernie, who I watch disappear into the house to help her mother. I had planned to tell her so many things.

It is dark and only a few people remain. I find Cheno and Bernie in the living room, sharing a pitcher of beer. He is holding it for her to drink from and she gulps and giggles. She is beyond drunk. He looks at me like he's about to rip me off again, and he whispers in her ear loud enough for me to hear, "Wanna get out of here?" Her hair flies up and then down from the strength of her nod.

"You can't leave yet, Bernie, you gotta help with all the food." I shut my eyes at my mistake.

"You wanna help us?" Bernie pokes Cheno's belly. "Let's go help."

"Oh, no, no, we have plenty of help." I try to cover.

"No sense, we'll help. Look at Cheno's big strong arms." Bernie squeezes his forearms and he smiles.

Bernie opens her arms toward the kitchen with its dishes, cups, overflowing trash sacks. "Wow, we made a mess."

"You gonna help me with my mess?" Bernie places her arm around Cheno's waist.

"Your what, mi amor?" Cheno holds her up.

"Mess, payaso." Bernie slaps at him.

"Oh, yes, I can help. One size fits all."

Bernie pats her chest and her breasts jiggle. "Yeah, I'll bet." Bernie flutters her eyes at me. I eye him like a snake waiting for a rat to eat.

"Where do we start?" Cheno rests his hand on her lap.

"In the back. Start collecting all the trash." I hand him a green plastic bag.

"The backyard?" Cheno stands, takes the bag, and shakes it in Bernie's face.

She giggles and stands. "Let's go." She trips into Cheno's arms. They embrace and Bernie is staring at Cheno's lips. I won't be getting any help from them.

"It's a shame we didn't get to dance," Cheno chuckles, and he sets the trash bag on the coffee table and caresses Bernie's arm to her wrist. He keeps hold of Vicente's gold bracelet with his fingers.

"There is no dancing at funerals." I look at Cheno.

He stares right back and then at Bernie's wrist. "Oh, well, yes, that makes sense."

My thoughts race, like a lizard being hunted, trying to figure out how to get him away from her, when Sal walks into the house from the backyard. I let out a sigh of relief.

"Start packing. Graciela's got the dually parked right outside." He points with both thumbs behind him. He takes the large aluminum tin tray of meat and walks back out the sliding door. "Andale, bro, get moving. You too, borracha," he tells Bernie, who giggles.

Cheno lets Bernie go and walks into the kitchen and lifts a case of Cokes, then walks out the door, and Bernie grabs his shirt and trails behind like a puppy.

Outside, moths and flying bugs buzz around the head- and tail-lights of Graciela's candy-red dually. Sal loads the food onto the bed of the truck, and I squeeze through the gate before Cheno and Bernie and past Graciela, who is heading toward the front yard to get her mother inside.

The *ping, ping* of the open door is steady. Inside the cab, I notice two purses in view and place them both under the driver-side seat just as Cheno and Bernie open the passenger-side door.

"We're helping, we're helping," Cheno says as Bernie kisses his cheek.

"Yes, yes, of course." I shut the door and watch him. "Bernie can ride up front with her mom, yeah?"

He throws the case of Cokes into the bed of the pickup, then kisses Bernie on the lips. "She's coming home with me."

Bernie points in his face. "No, you're coming home with me." She shakes the keys to her car in front of his face. He grabs them.

I let out a sigh and watch Bernie skip toward the street. Cheno is already inside her car. Graciela and her mother are walking toward me. Bernie stops, turns around, and skips up to them to give them hugs and kisses.

"Pórtate bien," her mother tells her.

"Don't." Graciela laughs and so does Bernie. She winks and gives me a flirtatious wave, and I smile.

Cheno stands on top of the landscape rocks with the Road Runner door open, swaying a little. "Are you coming, or not?"

Bernie gives Graciela one last squeeze and glances over at Cheno, who is bunching up his sleeves. He hangs his forearm over the car door.

"Hold on, sí?" She lifts a hand.

"Orale," Cheno replies.

She runs up to me and gives me a warm embrace. "This is a sign too. St. George's grass is greener than it's ever been."

I hug her back and she walks toward her blue muscle car. He

slaps her butt and she jumps a bit, then gets into the driver-side door.

"Meep, meep," he laughs. "I love this car."

"Let's go to my house." Bernie hugs Cheno's neck as he slams the door shut.

"Tell me where." He tells her loud enough for us hear as he places the key in the ignition.

"You know, your brother's old one," Bernie laughs.

"It's just a block over. Good." Cheno puts the car in reverse and floors it. The wheels screech and Señora Gomez looks up.

"Travieso," she says.

Graciela and I nod.

Señora Gomez stops in front of me and takes my hand. She says, "You're a good girl. I'm sorry about your mother and the cancer. She was a generous woman. She helped me when Graciela was born. Sent money when Vicente couldn't."

My tears fall on my silk top and I don't stop them.

"You look like her. And Bernadette tells me you love too much como Vicente."

"No." I wipe my eyes with my fingers.

"Como no." She winks at me. "You be good to your little girl." She pats my stomach.

"How do you know?"

"It's always a girl after twins." She fumbles in her purse for something and pulls out a purple bag that reads Crown Royal. She opens it and takes out a small square tin. "This is for you. Bury him, all of him, next to Josie. He always wanted to be American."

I am blinded by my tears. Gracey wraps her arms around me as Señora Gomez holds my hand.

SHORT STORIES

Shelf Life

TRINI LOPEZ CLOSED her eyes and sighed as she opened the prefab door to Adriana's room. Inside, seventy-year-old Alonso
pointed a charcoal pencil at her thirteen-year-old daughter.
Trini pinched the skin under her lower lip and tried to act
casual. Questions swirled like tiny dust devils in her head, but
she remained calm and collected. Why was Alonso inside her
house? How long had he been here? How long had these two
known each other? How much had they talked? How much had
he told her? She pinched harder when she noticed Adriana's
desk and dresser in the middle of the place, stacked with her
stuffed animals, clothes, and books. Adriana wasted too much
of her life on those dusty, worn, and dog-eared books. And now
the books were going to waste *her* time, she thought. Instead of
getting ready for her date, like she had planned on the hot,
sticky drive home, she was going to have to skip her shower and
make due with her work clothes. Her lip ached and she let it go
as she surveyed the wall that was cleared of pictures and post-
ers. She eyed the four straight, black horizontal lines drawn
across the length of it.

"How long has Alonso been here?" Trini's black high heels
coated with fine sand from outside left miniature crop circles in
the plush carpet.

"He just got here," Adriana said.

115

"Mucho gusto, señora." Alonso touched his finger to the brim of his painter's cap.

Trini nodded and her pale cheeks turned red. Her daughter's stern gaze and Alonso's presence made it feel like Adriana's father was there in the room. Adriana had the judgmental tilt of her father's chin and the strong set of his jaw. It took all Trini had not to walk over and slap the child. She resigned herself to being late.

"What's the problem?" Trini tried to sound like she knew what was going on.

Alonso, dressed in white overalls, waved the pencil at Adriana. "Your hija don't hear too good."

Adriana bounced up from her bed where she was sitting and pointed to herself with both thumbs. "He's trying to cheat me." A stack of yellow paperback books slid off a fleece blanket, littering the carpet.

"What the hell are you two talking about?" Trini rested her hands on her thin hips and her gold spangle bracelets rang. She eyed the jagged hole Adriana had made in the leather belt she wore. She cursed herself for not throwing it out, and for now seeing it cinching her daughter's too-big jeans. When Adriana rooted it out of the closet and Trini told her it belonged to Efren, the kid cherished it like a girl showing off an engagement ring.

Alonso pantomimed the letter "L" with his arms. "Quiere estant—"

"Shelves? What the hell do you want shelves for?" Trini peered down at Adriana as if the noon sun were shining in her eyes.

"For my books." Adriana dropped to her knees and collected the *Little House on the Prairie* series on the floor. "I've been saying. Telling you."

Fighting off the urge to yell, Trini pointed a manicured nail downward. "You're not getting any shelves." That's what the fucking floor is for, she thought.

"You said I could." Adriana looked up.

Trini shook her head, walked toward the kid, and placed a hand on her daughter's back. "Alonso, lemme talk to my daughter alone, yeah?"

"Sí como no." He walked around the mess in the room away from the two and out the door.

Trini clenched the back of her daughter's shirt and pulled her up. "When? When did I ever say I had money lying around to give you?"

Adriana's feet were planted so solid in the carpet that her toes were covered by the burgundy fibers. "Last night. You told me last night."

"You mean when I came in at three? Three in the morning?" She released Adriana's top and dug her fingers into her own hips. "Are you kidding me?"

"But I need them." Adriana set the paperbacks at the foot of her bed and then shrugged a shoulder toward the middle of the room.

Trini glanced in the direction Adriana motioned. A shining blue *American Heritage Dictionary* sat on top of the stack of books on the dresser and she wanted to knock it to the floor. She had bought it for Adriana last Christmas and she felt then, like she did now, confused and caught off guard. Trini remembered telling Alonso at the bar, when he handed her the brown sack with the book, "What kind of kid asks for a dictionary for Christmas? What the hell is wrong with her? Why doesn't she ask for a curling iron or clothes? God knows she could use them." Alonso had laughed and asked to meet her. He had said Adriana sounded exactly like Efren, always wanting to know. Trini's thoughts had raced all over the place like a moth in daylight as she sipped her drink. She needed one now. Alonso had talked so easily about Efren. He had told her he could ask Efren to help her out. Make him even. Alonso had said that it was a matter of principle. Trini stuck to her own set of principles, and she had ignored all Alonso had said and any talk of Adriana's father. She had been proud of her daughter for wanting a dictionary that could help her with schoolwork, but also angry because the girl wasn't like her cousins, and a little afraid of her strong-willed nature. Trini couldn't understand Adriana's need to know.

The rap on the door startled Trini. "What?"

"Discúlpeme, señora?" Alonso spoke as he opened the door. "I already bought tho wood. It's in my truck. I've started the job."

Trini looked up at the wall as if she were seeing it for the first time. Her lips parted, and a sound escaped like the click of a beer can opening. "Shit," she said under her breath as she looked from Alonso to Adriana.

Her irritation grew as she remembered how Adriana had tricked her into having a birthday party when she was just eight years old. Like these shelves, Trini had known Adriana had wanted the party, but she did not want her daughter to know that she couldn't afford it. Back then her father, Efren, still wasn't admitting the kid was his. When Adriana had asked for a party one last time before going to school, all Trini had said was, "You should have told me earlier." How could she have guessed that Adriana would use her time in class to write twenty-three birthday invitations and would hand them out at school? At home Adriana had handed Trini one of the cards she had made out of construction paper in the shape of a teddy bear. Trini's heart had seemed to foam in panic. "'Driana, who did you give this to?" she had asked. And the girl had said, "Everybody." She had asked her again, "Who, Dri? Tell me who. How many?" She had said, "Everybody in my class," with that unmoving and challenging glare that reminded Trini of Efren. Trini had wanted to drive Adriana to her father's doorstep that minute, but she doubted that her car could have made it up the mountain, so she had yanked Adriana's arm so hard that the girl tripped as she was being led outside. "You're lucky I already bought a birthday cake. Now we need to get all these pinche games, prizes, plates, and party hats." In the car, Trini had wanted to smile at Adriana, who sat smug in the bucket seat, rubbing her shoulder and looking like she had caught the eye of a man.

She had the same look now.

"Alonso's going to cover all the black marks." Adriana patted the air around her mother's back. "Don't worry, Mom. It'll even increase the value of the house when you sell it. He said."

"We're not selling our house." She peered out of the corner of her eye at Adriana's hands, which made Adriana lower them.

Alonso pointed the pencil at his chest and left a black mark on his white shirt. "I'm not doing no more work until you pay me what you owe." He gave Trini a wink.

"I already paid you!" Adriana stepped toward Alonso.

He looked down at her and grinned.

Trini checked her charm bracelet watch and with a sigh said, "How much does she owe you?"

"One hundred dollars." Alonso put his hands behind his back.

"You just finished telling me two." Adriana pointed.

Alonso stifled a laugh. "For la señora, since we work together, I'll knock a few dollars off." He stuck the pencil in the air like he was trying to hit a bull's-eye on a dart board.

"You trust him?" Adriana put her hands on her hips and they slid down to her thighs. "First, he tells me to pay him when the job is finished, and then he shows up early and says he wants money for supplies."

Trini stared in disbelief at Adriana. Stunned and awed at the power of emotions the kid brought out of her. Principle, a matter of principle, was what Alonso always said whenever Trini refused his requests to meet Adriana. She half expected the words to come out of Adriana's mouth. She wished Efron had principles when it came to his daughter. She looked at Alonso and rubbed her temples with her middle fingers. "How much have you given him, Adriana?"

"Twenty dollars," Alonso said as he took his cap off and ran a hand through his gray curls.

"Let's get one thing straight." Trini bent down to look at Adriana at eye level. "I'm giving him the money to finish these shelves, but you're not getting a Christmas gift or anything, not even clothes for school. Got it?"

Adriana's eyebrows arched and she fought the smile forming on her lips. "No problem, Mom. I don't need anything else. I really appreciate it. But . . ."

"What?" Trini stood straight and smoothed her hands over her fitted skirt down to her knees, trying to compose herself.

Adriana rubbed her hand over the leather belt at her waist and wiped her nose with the back of her hand.

Trini caught hold of her forearm and gripped it so that the girl sucked air. "I don't know, or care, how you found him, but I'm telling you now, you stay out of my papers, my business. My boss won't like Alonso working a side job."

"You said he's the best carpenter that 'stupid man' ever hired." Adriana didn't try to squirm or wriggle away.

Alonso laughed out loud.

Trini smiled at Adriana's direct quote, then frowned when she realized that she was keeping her boss waiting. "Alonso's a good man. He does good work. He'll be worth it. You can trust him. We can."

Adriana smiled as she stepped away from Trini. "He knows my dad, doesn't he?"

"Do anything like this again, and I will slap you so hard it'll knock all your teeth out. Got it?" She released Adriana and straightened up. "I'll deal with Alonso from now on."

There was a joy in Adriana's eyes that made her look drunk. Trini checked her watch again. She walked around the mess in the room, kicked a paperback on the floor, and followed Alonso out. She slammed the door shut, set her forehead against the particleboard, and wondered how Adriana was ever going to find herself a man. She felt Alonso's rough familiar hands on her back and sighed.

"She's just like m'ijo," he whispered, then laughed. "No te preocupes. I won't charge you, but let me do this for her. I won't tell her anything about him."

A River of Misunderstanding

PAUL GETS A halfie thinking about Sylvia's body. He wonders if she is watching him from behind. Below the bridge they walk on, he eyes the current of the río and notices how it makes a V in the water; this reminds him of Sylvia's hips and belly. He doesn't slow down, remembering what he's been told. As Paul walks and watches the rising sun poke the purple mountains awake, he thinks of her, and he smiles. In front of him, the Franklins, fat with life, are open, expansive, and welcoming. The air is still. There is no sand blowing in his face to sting his eyes.

"Straighten up," Sylvia says.

He laughs because he knows he looks like a question mark, then he straightens. Like this, he sees several yards over everyone. Erect, he stands a foot above the short, black-haired people on the international bridge that connects Juárez to El Paso. He is glad that he is American, so there is no waiting. Mexicans stand in a long line to his right. Paul can't wait to get Sylvia alone, and he can't believe she is still into him after three weeks. He sets his beer-tinted sight on the glass double doors of the border checkpoint. He wants to get to the other side. His mouth waters thinking about the too-hot menudo at the Good Luck Cafe, retreating into his dorm room, and crawling into bed with Sylvia. He wants to wait for her, hold her hand, and touch her hair, ears, cheeks, lips, but he remembers his father's words, "calm and cool." His thoughts and his erection grow muddy like the water below. His body bends back into its natural, uncertain, doubtful position, and Paul does not stand out anymore.

"Wait up. I'm gonna throw up if you don't slow down," Sylvia says.

Paul feels a tug at his belt loop and his crotch. Her breath is heavy and he stiffens again.

"Keep up." He picks up the pace, and he no longer feels her pull on his pants. He has to stop himself from looking back. He doesn't want to get too far ahead. All he can hear is the knocking of wooden soles on pavement, the clicking of heels, the squeaking of plastic sandals, the ruffling of bags, and the chattering of Mexicans and Americans. He wants to watch Sylvia's short, wiry legs taking three steps to every one of his own, but he wants to play it cool too. The advice his father gave is still working with her. He worries she may be too drunk to speak to the guard at the turnstiles, and he feels a bit nauseated himself. "Hurry up or you'll be lost in Mexico," he says.

"What? Will you slow down?" The honking horns and increasing distance between them drown out the rest of Sylvia's response.

Paul eyes the chrome guardrails to his left. He's going to stick to his plan. His father is right; being apendejado over women hasn't gotten him anywhere. But Sylvia does make Paul stupid. She's beautiful. He is thankful that the rails can protect her from the angry drivers revving their car engines while they idle, impatient to cross. He wonders if the cement and chain link fence can bear the weight of so many standing against it. The row of people ends at the bronze placard that marks the border above the Rio Grande and snakes all the way to the double doors on the American side. It's about the distance of the field in Texas Stadium. The men in line look tired but stand. The majority of the women and children sit on the hot concrete. All have their belongings next to them in sacks, suitcases, or bags. The walkers to his left carry plastic bags stretched so full they are translucent; a few bump him, and he can hear Sylvia's distant yells of "excuse me" and "watch it" to people passing her by.

Paul stops midstride because he recognizes a face in line. He ducks his head and doesn't dare look behind him. It is his aunt Bertha. She is sitting on a light-blue suitcase a few yards ahead of him and wearing his mother's old green cocktail dress with a pink bag on her lap. He doesn't want Sylvia to see her, the dress, or the old, dirty suitcase, so he rushes toward Bertha in an effort to lose Sylvia. As if he called out to her, she looks up, sees him a few feet away, and smiles wide. Bertha's grin shows her front missing tooth and the three light-brown ones on either side of the gap. Paul closes his eyes and wills her to stop showing her bad teeth. He wishes Sylvia had been in front of him, so she couldn't see her, or him, all of them together. He wades with the traffic of people toward Dertha, thinking about how he can make a fast getaway. As he crosses the tide of bodies, Bertha nudges his cousins on either side of her and points toward Paul. In turn, they prod the little ones, who sit Indian style next to them. Paul reaches the group and eyes the kids, who look sleepy but stand obediently.

"Paulino, what a miracle to see you, and you are still so handsome, the spitting image of your father," Bertha says in Spanish, standing with her large arms in the air, open, ready. She embraces him quickly and traps his arms at his sides.

An embarrassed giggle escapes Paul's mouth, and he rests his cheek on the top of her head in return.

"Aunt, uh, tía, uh, Bertha st—, sto—, stop." He can't get the words in Spanish out and moves away from Bertha's embrace.

Bertha holds on to Paul, massaging and caressing his arms as if he is cold. "Our trip has been long. We woke up at one in the morning and traveled from the fraccionamiento to catch the bus and it was running late, but this is not news. The children found seats but we had to stand for the hour-long ride, and it dropped us at Cuauhtémoc Square. Someday I'd like to see a movie there. We walked the rest of the way and made it to the bridge by four."

Paul can feel Sylvia's tug at his belt loop and he steps away from her toward his aunt. He lets out a breath when he no longer feels her grip on his pants. He notices that Bertha nods at Sylvia behind him.

"I am sorry the trip was so long," Paul says in perfect Spanish, then he cuts the air with his hand. "Do you have a ride to the house of Rolando once you get across?"

"You speak Spanish?" Sylvia tugs at the hem of Paul's football jersey.

He didn't want Sylvia to know that he speaks Spanish. Sylvia's English is perfect. She doesn't know any Spanish; she has no trace of an accent. God, and his Spanish, he thinks.

"Oh, no, no, no, the trip was not so long and we can finally rest." Bertha smiles and glances over Paul's shoulder. "Hello. What a pretty girl you are. What beautiful hair you have. Are you the girlfriend of Paul?"

"What is she saying?" Sylvia lets go of the jersey. "Paul?"

Bertha pats Sylvia's shoulder. "Oh, she speaks no Spanish. What a shame." She focuses on Paul. "By the looks of the line, we will cross over in a few hours; we are coming only for a short visit this time, a few weeks only, and, maybe, Ivonne can find some work here; she irons better than the machine at the cleaners, Rolando always says when we are here. Maribel might want some work, but she won't be able to keep a job because already she is a month along."

Ivonne and Maribel exchange looks behind her back and giggle.

"What beautiful dresses," Sylvia says. "How do you manage to look so good in this heat?"

Ivonne, Maribel, and Bertha look at Paul and wait.

Paul feels his face hot. He can't look Ivonne and Maribel in the eyes, so he looks at the sidewalk instead. He's humiliated by the fact that they are wearing his sister's old clothes and Maribel even has on her white high heels.

"Those shoes make your calves look great," Sylvia says.

A group of drunk Americans walk in the middle of the conversation and force everyone to step away from each other.

He sees Maribel smile and look down at her feet. Paul knows they are being polite and not regarding Sylvia until he gives her a proper introduction.

"I will tell my mother that you arrived safely," he says in a smooth, quick sentence, his voice steady. "It's good to see everyone. I will tell my mother that you are here and safe."

The women look at one another, then at Paul, and then at each other again. With a frown Bertha says, "God bless you, Son. Later, we will visit more."

"I should get home now. It was good to see everybody." He pats the boy, whose name he doesn't say, on the head. "Can I take anything across for you? Maybe a bag or two so you won't have to carry them or get them inspected?"

"No, Son, we don't want to *burden* you with our things." She tilts her head at Sylvia behind Paul.

"You are, um, I mean, it's no burden at all," Paul says.

Bertha reaches for Paul's arm, but she stops herself and says, "It would be best if we declared all we had because the Border Patrol agents are probably watching us right now. What if something of ours does not pass? What a burden it would be for you. Imagine me explaining to my sister-in-law why the migra is holding her son. What a *burden* we would be."

Sylvia brushes past Paul as she walks north.

He says, "Well, good-bye and God bless you." He bends and gives his aunt a proper hug this time. He squeezes hard, trying to erase the hurt he heard in her tone, his anger, and his shame. "I will see everyone soon—tía, Maribel, Ivonne, Epifino, Soledad." Paul embraces his cousins and pats the children, who snuggle his legs. Paul looks ahead at Sylvia's hair that seems to sparkle golden in the sun. "Good-bye." He gives a two-fingered salute and steps into the foot traffic. He is grateful that Sylvia didn't force an introduction. He hopes that she saw, like he did, how they looked like poor people in party clothes.

Sylvia swings her arms like a soldier marching forward. She is halfway to the checkpoint and he has to jog to catch up. Before he can touch it, she opens the double door, squeezes herself in, and lets it shut behind her. He will tell her how he is nothing like them. How he doesn't see them but once every few months. He can explain it to her. Maybe he shouldn't explain, because talking hasn't worked in the past. His father said, "Men should be quiet and strong." He wishes he could ask his father what to do. He's just barely treading water. Through the door he watches her advance toward the turnstiles that are guarded by a man wearing a thick green uniform with a leather belt and a brass buckle.

When Paul opens the door, he lets three people file in before him. Inside, he walks on linoleum so clean even the darkest person looks light skinned. He shakes his head when he sees Sylvia's right hand on her hip. The people he allowed through wave for Paul to get in line in front, so he is behind Sylvia. He nods a thank-you and takes his place. He wants to touch Sylvia, but that hand on her hip makes him put his own in his pocket.

"American, and I have nothing to declare," Sylvia says, not waiting for the guard. She pushes at the stainless-steel arm of the turnstile. It doesn't budge. She pushes again, and it doesn't move. She looks up at the guard, who winks and smiles, presses something behind a steel box, then waves her through. Another shove by Sylvia and the arm turns; she forges ahead, then struggles to force the automatic doors open.

The guard says, "What's your nationality?"

"'Merican," Paul says.

"Do you have anything to declare?"

"Nothing."

The guard's gold name tag shines under the fluorescent light; Espinosa in block letters flashes for a second. He whispers, "She's white hot. Good luck keeping that one."

Outside, Sylvia waits for cars to pass before she can cross the street.

Paul reaches her and touches her elbow. "What's wrong?"

She pulls her arm away from his touch and looks up at him. "What's wroooong? You have to ask?"

Her red-rimmed eyes tell him what he already knows. Still, he says, "Syl, I don't know if you don't tell me."

126

"Paul, how do you think I felt standing there?" She nods toward the port of entry. "While you talked to your family, I was standing behind you the entire time and you didn't even introduce me. You didn't even look at me. I didn't even know you speak Spanish."

He looks into her far-reaching, bloodshot eyes, sighs, then pulls at his curls near the back of his neck. This is it, he thinks. We're over. She's not going to want someone like me, someone who speaks Spanish, with family from Mexico.

"I'm not even good enough to be introduced to your own family!" she says in a too-high voice.

His mouth opens. His face gets red and he shoves his hands in his pockets to keep from grabbing her. The words "calm and cool" rush like currents in his head. He looks at the street in front of him. The sweat trickles down his back.

"God." Her lips tremble and she closes her eyes tight, rubs her forehead with her fist. "So it's true. Why? Why are we even together?"

"No, no, don't be stupid, Syl. That's not it at all." He continues looking at the street, while easing one hand out of his pocket and up the back of his neck. He wished he hadn't drunk so much at the Kentucky Club. How can he play it cool now? She wants him, really wants him. He rolls his eyes. "You got it all wrong."

"Now I'm stupid too?" She lifts her hands to shove Paul, but lets them drop to her sides. "Is it because you think I'm dumb that you didn't want your family to know who I am? So I'm just your dumb, fun girlfriend, is it?"

His mouth is so dry. He pulls at the hair near his neckline and winces. To avoid Sylvia's glare, he stares up at the blue sky. Remembering how he lost the seven other girlfriends with all his talk, he's going to get this one right. The wind picks up but his ideas stop. No thoughts, nothing but honking horns and revving engines. He is quiet, but he knows Sylvia wants something from him. Aloof, he decides.

"They had on those clothes." He points behind him.

"And so?" Both Sylvia's hands are fists.

"Those are their best clothes." He kicks a pebble of tar and can see the sand blow across the asphalt.

"Am I dressed wrong?" She punches her thighs. "Do I have to wear my best clothes to be introduced to your family?"

"No, Syl." He wonders how to tell her. How to explain. "I'm sorry. You look tired. You're eyes are all red. Let me—"

"Let you what? Insult me even more. You already called me stupid."

"No, no, that's not what I said." He scratches his head trying to figure it out. How she's got the wrong idea. She shouldn't cry. He wonders how to fix this. Would it be okay to touch her? It's what comes natural, but his father told him to do the opposite of natural. He doesn't want to mess this up. His father would know what to do. He takes a step toward her and runs his fingers over her arms, which are now crossed in front of her. She jerks away. "Syl, come on." He frowns, thinking she should know. She should know it's not her, because he holds her in his arms every night. Why doesn't she get it? They lie by each other, almost every night, every night. He listens to her dreams of leaving this desert for the California beach, and he holds her when she shakes from excitement of the things to come. She gets him excited too with all her happiness and big talk, and he wants to make love to her, but he doesn't; he waits and he listens. Plays it cool. Listens until the pitch of her voice softens and she takes breaths between sentences and allows him into her conversation, into her head, into her world, into her body. How can she be insulted?

Tears flow down Sylvia's cheeks. "Take me home."

"You don't want to come over?" He tries to touch her again.

"Oh, stop it!" She waves her arms until he puts his hands in his pockets. "Stop it, will you?" She stands still. "Just take me home."

He kicks the ground before deciding to go get the car. Slumped, he crosses the street into the shining river of bumpers, hoods, and windshields. Sweat trickles from his hairline, and he looks up. The sun overhead colors the mountains orange and each peak looks razor sharp and he can feel grit on his teeth.

Addressed

MY MOTHER HAS been gone for an hour and I don't want to call everyone with the news, but I have to. I sit on this plastic green bucket seat in the sterile hallway of the hospital and run my fingers over the beige-colored dividers, trying to remember if my mother labeled her sister's phone number under "V" for Vanessa or "S" for sister. When I flip the gilt-edged pages searching for my aunt's phone number the information isn't in either place. It's just like her to make things more difficult. She never does what is practical, easy. I've told her countless times, "Normal people order their address book by the first letter in a person's last name. All you need to do is look inside the phone book." Mom usually says, "That's why you can't find anything in that stupid book." I snort a laugh and shake my head, then press my fingers on the dividers until they bend. Why can't she just use things the way they were meant to be used? Is that so difficult for her to understand? Was that so difficult? Why was it such a hard thing for her to do? I flip to the letter "T" and rip the wax paper–thick page near the bottom. "T" for tía, aunt in Spanish, and there is Aunt Vanessa's phone number, directly above Aunt Dee Dee's. I stare at the looped letters of my mother's writing until my eyes blur wet. I shut the pocketbook and clutch its shiny periwinkle-blue cover so that it bends in my grip. Tears fall on the gold lettering that reads "Bonnie Archuleta." I run my fingers across the engraved letters to wipe the drops off but also to touch her name, as if that will bring her closer to me, bring her back.

In a way it does. I can remember her at the flea market when I was a kid. We would always stop by the booth filled with cheap vinyl-covered books. It had calendars, address books, Bibles, journals, and planners in pink, yellow, white, baby blue. All the colors people would not buy. A one-legged man ran the Easter booth, which is what we'd call it. He perched next to the books on a tall stool with only one back spindle. His engraving-machine cart, made from an old popcorn maker, sat on the other side of him. When someone wanted a book engraved he would spin around, open the doors to the popcorn maker, and suggest to the person that they stand on the other side to watch him work. From the other side through the glass was a view of the top of his head, with thick, black hair, and vials filled with colored powders lining the bottom of the glass. In the kettle, where the popcorn should go, he kept an electric drill and needles of varying widths and sizes. He would plug his electric drill into the fat orange power cord and dip the needle, fashioned out of an ice pick or a knife, into a vial, and time would stand still. He worked with the slow precision of a scientist splitting atoms, careful and deliberate because he could not read.

I watched him mess up a customer's order, once, when he was in a hurry. He drew an "S" so that it looked like the number two. I remember thinking that adults shouldn't make the same mistakes I did with their letters. The man, Severino, whose name I learned from sounding it out where he wrote it on a piece of cardboard, demanded his five dollars back. The engraving scientist counted out five dollars from a small wad of bills he took out of his jean pocket. He straightened them and laid them flat on Severino's callused palm. Severino bunched them up in his fist and marched away. My mother had been watching too. She picked up a book from his display, one with a white cover, and laid it in front of the man, then took the cardboard with Severino's name, flipped it over, crossed out the names Chuy and Roberta, and wrote Carmen Archuleta in large block letters for the man to copy. The engraver smiled, took the cardboard, propped it against the back glass of the popcorn machine so that I had to stand on tiptoes to see him work, and began engraving. When he finished, my name was printed in gold, glittery letters underneath the title *Nuevo Testamento: Salmos Y Proverbios*. Mom had no idea she had picked up a Bible.

"Veinte dolares," he had said to her.

Mom had gasped. "Are you crazy?"

He shook his head then said in perfect English, "The word of God has no price."

Mom looked over to me then at the man. "I feel that way, exactly," she said, and handed him a ten-dollar bill.

He took it without a word. She shoved the book in my hands and walked toward a booth of socks. I stood there for a minute and opened the book in the middle to Psalms, and I realized it was written in Spanish. At eight years old, I was just getting the hang of reading English, but I kept the book. It was the first and only one my mother bought me.

I grip the address book and shake my head at the memory. I lower my eyes whenever someone passes by in the hallway. I notice that the golden "A" in Archuleta on the cover is slanted like on my Spanish-language New Testament and I shut my eyes tight. This address book in my hand is brand new, as if my mother were planning for today. Throughout the years she had always asked me why I didn't just throw the Bible away. Said she hated the gaudiness of it. When I told her because she bought it for me, she would sigh. That sound could only mean one of two things: either she was getting ready to yell at someone or she was pleased. She was like that, my mother, either high or low, no in between. She never made me throw the Bible out, even when it was smeared with black fingerprints. It's that Mom hated dirt, filth, the hint of it, the sight of it, the idea of it. I can remember stumbling into the bathroom late at night and seeing her there on her knees scrubbing the toilet bowl with a rag, muttering, "No one is ever going to call me dirty." When Mom would clean my room, after I'd done a poor job of it, she would take care to place the white New Testament in the exact spot where I had left it. The smudges would be wiped away and it would smell like the rest of the house, like acidic pine, similar to this hospital where I sit. The tacky Bible was our secret language of love. Whenever Mom needed to hear something sweet or feel good she would start harping about my filthy Bible, the dusty book with its ugly cover. "Throw it away," she would say. I would reply, "Never, because you gave it to me." It was our shorthand for "I love you," without actually having to admit it.

Here it is again, the shorthand, in this pale-blue address book I hold. I am sure she bought it from Severino at the flea market. There is no mistaking the color. She bought it specifically for this day. A day I've dreaded since she was diagnosed. In my mother's cockeyed way, she picked this address book just for me. To help me through having to call everyone, my ex-stepdad, my aunts and uncles, my grandparents, her friends, boyfriends. She knew that I would keep this book, not because it is my favorite color, but because *she* left it for me.

I can't bring myself to call aunt Vanessa so I look up my ex-stepfather, Zachary Smith. I look under "C" for cabrón and he is the second person listed. The first is her brother, Uncle Manny. I chuckle and wipe my eyes with my free hand, trying to decide if she had put him under "C" because he liked to eat cabrito or because he was a cabrón too. Tío Manny was always sleeping around on my aunt Dee Dee, who Mom called Tonta. The nickname stuck, and everyone in the family called Dee Dee Ton for short.

I laugh out loud when I realize Mom put Dee Dee under "T" with Vanessa, not because she's my aunt but because of the nickname, Ton. A nurse walking by in scrubs smiles. Her flirty mouth reminds me of Mom. I check under "D" for daughter, looking for my name within the pages, but only see her gay friend Osvaldo, who she refers to as a "plumita" or "that dog." I flip through the pages carefully now toward the back of the book, to the "Ws" for "whiner." She always called me that because I hated to clean. Still do. I didn't understand why everything had to look a certain way, smell a certain way, look brand new, unused, and I told her so. I sit up. Worried that she didn't put me in this, her last address book, I decide to read it like an ordinary book, beginning on page one. I open it and read, "This address book belongs to Bonnie Archuleta," in her jagged, thin scrawl. Her address and phone number were probably penned in a hurry. I can tell by the way they tilt right as if running off the page. The next sheet begins the "A" tab, and there I am, the first entry, right at the top of the page—Carmen Archuleta.

stupids

stupid america, see that chicano . . .

I'M IN THIS stupids class. We're all here again, me with my bad attitude, and the two other dumb Mexicans. Whatever. Jimmy is here like usual, and I'm not gonna bother saying hey because he don't talk. Turi's here. That guy talks too much. I'm gonna sit next to the windows opposite Jimmy and far enough in front of Turi, so I can't hear him in the back. He's pretty smart, just annoying as hell with all his moving around and mumbling. I know I'm not stupid, my dad knows it too. And I know that my mom knows now. I saw it in her face when I had my foot on her throat after she threw an egg sandwich at me. When she realized I wasn't going to take her shit the way Dad did, she split real quick. I thought she'd be home by the end of the summer for sure, but we haven't seen her since. Dad finally got steady work because he doesn't have to call in sick anymore. Even though he doesn't tell me, I can tell he's glad about her being gone too. Can't wait to get home to eat the beans or lengua burritos he leaves for me in the frigerator for after school. God, I hate school. It's such a waste. I could be working full-time. I hate these desks. My body doesn't fit. The steel bars feel like they're welded into the side of my thigh, and the damn wire bookrack rings every time my shoes hit it, pretty much any time I move. Ignore it. Don't think and the eight hours will fly by.

I like the colors on the map of El Paso in the front of the room. Pretty cool, it looks almost 3-D. Whoa, that must be Mr. Hernandez. He's big, taller than me. I wonder what he's gonna be like. I never had a dude for a teacher. He's got to be better than my other teachers, or at least different. I like that he doesn't wear a suit like the only other guy on campus. Hernandez looks all right. I mean at least he didn't look at me like the others do. Their stares remind me of how Dad would look at Mom when she was being an asshole. I wanna scream at them like Mom screams at Dad. I wonder how they make El Paso look like it's popping out of the map? The city of the pass, more like the city *to* pass. I laugh out loud at my joke.

"Quiet." Mr. Hernandez knocks his huge knuckle against the chalkboard behind him.

I wish I could tell Turi my rhyme. He'd love it, but I can't because he'd jump up and down and probably repeat it out loud like he does. Great, here comes Principal Morgan with his suit and tie, looking all official for the "listen here, dumbasses" speech.

He's raising his hands like there's thirty and not just three of us in here.

"Listen here, people." He claps and points to Mr. Hernandez, who is sitting in a chair behind the desk. "This is Mr. Hernandez. He's a new teacher this year, so I want you to be on your best behavior."

Why is he looking at me when he says this? Fuck him.

"We are lucky to have him here with us. He has a degree from Arizona State in history. He's traveled abroad and has been stationed in Germany for the last five years. He lives here now, in Fort Bliss."

I think of Dad and how he says that only poor Mexicans and gringos would actually *choose* to live in El Paso. I wonder if Mr. Hernandez is poor. Finally, Morgan is gone, but not before one last stare down. Mr. Hernandez is up from behind his desk. I wonder where he got acid-wash bellbottoms? They'd look better straight leg like Jimmy's wearing. He pulls a map down like a window shade and covers the colored one I was looking at. It's a map of Texas and Mexico.

He says, "The City of the Pass."

I sit up because I was just making fun of that. This is a trip. The ping from the bookrack echoes. Wonder why this map has a red line from Mexico City, through El Paso all the way up to New Mexico? Who's the medieval-looking dude in armor right next to El Paso? There it is again, "The City of the Pass" printed on the top in blocky cholo letters. Wonder what this could mean?

"This is Don Juan de Oñate." Mr. Hernandez touches the dude in armor, then points at Turi, who is waving his arm high.

"Is he the dude that gets all the chicks in the movies?" Turi says, all out of breath sounding.

Mr. Hernandez laughs. "No, Arturo. He's the dude who discovered El Paso. He's the dude who discovered the narrow passageway through the Franklin Mountains into North America. He's the dude who used God to justify killing hundreds, maybe even thousands, of Mexicanos and Indios right here in the Southwest. Mexicanos who looked just like us."

I don't mind Mr. Hernandez's sarcastic tone or that he's laughing at Turi, or even that he knows our names already, like he's been talking about us behind our backs, because I can't believe what he just said about using God to kill Mexicans. I picture priests stabbing Turi and Jimmy in the chest with crosses. These priests in my head look like the Mormons who Dad and me hide from in the house when they come to the door. They make me so mad. Don't they once think that if we wanted to go to a church, we would already be there? And come to think of it, it's always white people that come to our door, bugging. This Oñate he's pointing at has gotta be white.

I look over at Jimmy and fuck if he isn't raising his hand. The guy never even talks, let alone raises his hand in a class. I didn't think he even knew English. I wanna hear him talk.

"Yes, Jimmy?" Mr. Hernandez pushes his sleeves up to his elbows like he's gonna work on a faucet or something.

"Oñate was Spanish, right? He's a white guy?" Jimmy asks.

Damn, the dude knows English and he knows who this knight is, too. He was thinking the exact same thing about Oñate that I was. Here I thought this morenito was a Mexicano and turns out he's American, like me, just looks Mexican. He doesn't even have an accent.

"Correct, Jimmy. You know some historians believe that the first Thanksgiving wasn't in Plymouth but right here in El Paso in 1598." Mr. Hernandez points to the floor.

Mr. Hernandez didn't even act surprised to hear Jimmy talk. I think he's gonna be pretty cool. Doesn't make a big deal out of it like the other teachers would, just moves on like nothing. Wait a minute. Did he just say Thanksgiving was here in El Paso? Jimmy raises his hand again and my head feels like it's about to explode because Jimmy is talking and also because I think this Mr. Hernandez is crazy. He must be to be talking to us like this. Mr. Hernandez points at him. This time I keep my eyes on Mr. Hernandez.

"I see that white dude on TV every year. You know the one?" Now Jimmy's pointing too.

"I think you're talking about Sherton Wall. He belongs to the El Paso Historical Society," Mr. Hernandez says.

"What's that?" Turi says, rubbing a hand over the back of his buzz cut as he paces.

Jimmy looks back at Turi. "It's bunch a white guys that like history; they hang out and eat."

"When did you get so smart?" I say before I can stop myself.

"I don't know about smart." Jimmy puts his head down and then looks up at Mr. Hernandez through his long bangs. "I work at Montezuma's downtown, and they all order from us. I deliver their food. They tip good."

"You work? Why isn't that in your records?" Mr. Hernandez stands up, walks behind his desk, and opens a red folder. All our folders are red. He looks through it a minute, sighs, and then tosses it. It lands quiet on top of the other red folders. He returns to the front of his desk. "How long have you been working?"

"I dunno, long as I can remember. Since I was twelve, eleven maybe. My boss, Mr. Zuniga, lets me eat all I want. He's all right. Sometimes if it's too late to catch the bus back home, he lets me sleep there."

"Oh, really?" Mr. Hernandez is shoving those sleeves almost up to his armpits. "Why doesn't anybody here know about this?"

"Ah, man, Mr. Zuniga told me not to tell nobody, because he pays me cash. You know, I'm not on the books." Jimmy scribbles in an imaginary notebook.

"So that's why you're always late to school." Mr. Hernandez rubs his chin. "Good to know, good to know."

"You're not gonna tell nobody, are you?" Jimmy looks scared.

Mr. Hernandez looks down to the floor, stands, then begins to pace like Turi. "No, I'm not telling anyone unless you want me to." He stops walking. "And neither is anyone in this class."

Turi raises his hand. "Yes, Arturo."

"So what do the good tippers do? Are they like a gang?"

Mr. Hernandez looks up at the light that is flickering above him. "Well, I guess you could call it a gang. Hey, Jimmy, turn off the light, yeah?"

"What are you doing, Mr. H?" Turi asks and walks up the aisle.

"It's Mr. Hernandez to you. I gotta change this bulb." Mr. Hernandez is standing on a desk next to mine and looking down. "Jennifer, will you give me a sheet of paper I can throw away, please."

I open my notebook, tear out a sheet, and hand it to him. He rips it in half and uses the paper like rags to jiggle the hot bulb from its sockets. He holds the long bulb in his hands over his head. "The historical society is a bunch of guys that like history, just like Jimmy said. They talk about it, El Paso history. Celebrate it. Turn on the light, please."

"Yeah, I seen 'em dressed up in armor like that Oñate," Jimmy says as he flicks the light on.

"They stage reenactments." Mr. Hernandez jumps off the chair holding the long bulb like he's about to whale on a piñata. "They reenact the first Thanksgiving."

"You mean like a play?" Arturo stands still. "I was an Indian in a Thanksgiving play in third grade."

"Well, yes and no. Remember how I was telling you about the first Thanksgiving being here in El Paso, and not Plymouth—

which is probably the play your class reenacted in elementary school?" Mr. Hernandez walks to a closet near the doorway. "The El Paso Historical Society members reenact the first Thanksgiving in El Paso. They get together and do this in San Elizario."

"Where's that?" Turi jumps from one foot to the other and slaps his open mouth.

"I've been there," Jimmy says. "That Sherton guy is all bald and the skin on his head is always peeling. He has a weird accent."

"It's because he's from New York," Mr. Hernandez says while opening a closet. "San Elizario is a few miles outside the city limits."

"Is it close to Western Playland?" Turi's hands are behind his back and he is marching slow.

"No, the opposite direction." Mr. Hernandez sets the used bulb on the floor, shuts the door and locks it with keys from his pocket. He walks to the map he pulled down and points to the right of the dot that says El Paso. "Right about here. Jimmy, what did you do there?"

"They paid me to help with the horses. But I wound up being a water boy."

"There are horses?" I ask.

"Yeah. I just pretty much loaded food for the horses and when the knights got overheated I started handing them cups of water."

Mr. Hernandez laughed. "I'll bet they get pretty hot in those iron suits."

"They could only wear 'em for like fifteen minutes at a time." Jimmy grinned. "I always wondered why they did it. The TV stations would come and film them, five white dudes on horses in armor in the middle of the day. I thought they were just stupid."

"What channel?" Turi asks as he does standing push-ups using two desks.

"I dunno." Jimmy looks back at him. "All of them."

"Man, I like watching channel nine. They got smoking hot white chicks reporting." Turi jumps out of the push-up, then looks at me.

Jimmy and Mr. Hernandez are staring at me too, like Dad would look at Mom when she was starting up. I feel like I'm supposed to say something.

"I dunno about that, but the dudes are ug-lee on channel nine." I shift in my seat and the damn rack pings.

They all laugh.

"Yeah, the chicks are hot if you like white girls," Jimmy says.

We're quiet, waiting for Mr. Hernandez to tell us to shut up, to tell us we are being rude, to tell us we're stupid. Instead, he's leaning on his desk nodding at us.

"I like 'em all." Turi does a spin.

"Too bad they don't like you," I say, and everyone laughs, even Mr. Hernandez.

Mr. Hernandez looks down at my feet and walks over to me. "Stand up, please."

I'm going to the principal's office for sure now. I'm sure I pissed him off, so I go ahead and walk toward the door before he can tell me.

"Where are you going?" Mr. Hernandez is moving my desk to the back of the class.

"To the principal's?"

"Why? You like Mr. Morgan?"

I watch Mr. Hernandez set the desk down and lift a small table that was in the corner of the room over his head. "Do you?"

"What are you doing?" Turi asks.

"Making this room more comfortable. We're stuck here for four hours all semester long." Mr. Hernandez huffs as he sets the table where my desk was.

"Jennifer, do me a favor and get the chair from my desk and bring it over here." He points to his desk.

I do what he asks.

He steps away to give me room. "See if this is any better. How tall are you?"

"I dunno, like six foot something," I say as I sit down.

"Yeah, I thought so. I'm six two and I've been this tall since seventh grade. These combo desks were made for average-sized students, not supermodel sizes."

I laugh out loud because nobody has ever called me a super-model—manflora, dyke, Lurch, but supermodel, never.

"Now, where were we?" He claps.

"Hot chicks," I say.

"Yes, you're right." Mr. Hernandez points at me.

"They're all good looking on TV." Turi reminds us as he walks.

"Not all," Jimmy says.

"Name one." Turi hangs on a desk.

"Brooke Ditchfield, Ashton Clark, and Amy Ryan."

"What do you got against white chicks?" I ask.

"Nothing," Jimmy says. "I just . . . I just . . . I dunno. They're all white on the news shows, so we watch Univision."

"I think what Jimmy is trying to articulate," Mr. Hernandez points at Jimmy, "and correct me if I'm wrong, Jimmy, the problem he's having isn't that he doesn't like 'white chicks' but that he hates that there are no brown ones on TV."

Jimmy's mouth opens and he nods.

"What do you mean, brown ones?" I say.

"You know, morenitas," Turi says and walks toward me. "Dark chicks that look more like you."

I look at my arms. "Shut up, I'm not that dark. I could pass."

Mr. Hernandez waves his hands toward me like he's introduc-ing me. "Case in point, you two just proved what is wrong with TV and why Jimmy can't really articulate what he hates about TV news here in El Paso. Nowhere else but in this forgotten part of West Texas would they hire white people from up North to deliver the news to half a million brown Americans and Mexicans."

No one talks for what seems like hours. We just sit. I feel caught like I imagine a lizard feels in my hand when I pick it up. Me and Dad watch channel nine every night when we eat. I watch Brooke Ditchfield and Marty Christiansen deliver the news. We laugh when they say Juárez and Porfirio Díaz streets all wrong, but I never thought that maybe someone else could do that stuff. I mean someone like me.

"I like to watch those reporters telling us that El Paso means 'The Pass' in Spanish," Mr. Hernandez says.

Turi paces and mutters, "Mr. Hernandez's saying some shit, saying some shit."

"How do you know so much about El Paso?" I ask.

"I was born and raised here. I've been listening to people, not from here, give us the news since 1941. First on the radio and newspaper, and now on TV, and it's still the same." Mr. Hernandez ignores us even though we all have our hands up. "Never mind that just half a mile away from where I stand, there are news offices on the other side of the border that have been in business for over a hundred years and have been delivering news to generations of brown people—"

"So, like, why don't the TV ever write about the cops and how they stop me and my brother for nothing?" Jimmy asks.

"Because they don't know about it." Mr. Hernandez is back to pushing his sleeves. "Nobody calls them and tells them this is happening. Have you ever called them?"

We all laugh.

"Yeah, right, like they'll listen," I say.

"It's part of your responsibility to do that."

I cross my arms because I can't decide if I should stop talking or tell him the truth. I shift in my seat and realize that the annoying ping is gone, so I talk. "My responsibility is to keep my family safe and to look after myself."

"Yes, you're right." Mr. Hernandez looks at me. "It's every man's responsibility to protect his family, and part of protecting family is letting the stupids at the newspaper know what is going on right under their noses. It's every, um, person's responsibility."

Second time in a row this man surprises me. It's like the *Twilight Zone*. I'm in another dimension, where everything makes sense. I look out the window to be sure the sun is still there before I answer, "I'm not gonna go to the papers. You crazy? The paper, school, cops, and government are all trouble. I'll get in trouble."

"No, you won't," Jimmy says. "They'll just ignore you. You gotta do what my mom does. Whenever she sees the cops messing with teenagers, she stops the car and parks. It don't matter if we're late or whatever. She gets out, sits on the hood, and watches them.

Some get all freaked out and come up to her and tell her to move along, 'This is police business,' but then she tells them, all pissed off, 'I'm not disturbing you or what you are doing. I'm just a citizen making sure those teenage boys are being treated fairly.'"

"Wow, your mom has a lot of balls," Turi says.

I nod. I can't imagine my mom doing something like that, because she hates cops so much she drives the other way when she sees one driving down the street. Dad? Dad won't even stand up to an asshole like Mom.

Jimmy smiles and looks down at his desk. "Yeah, some of the more assholish ones run her driver's license or whatever they do. It don't even bother me that we're late everywhere."

Jimmy looks up at Mr. Hernandez. Mr. Hernandez smiles wider, looks at the red folder on his desk, then nods his head.

Turi is putting his hands in his pockets and then pulling them out. "The TV should interview my cousin Monchie. He knows famous people; he knows Fats Domino."

"Monchie?" Mr. Hernandez crosses his arms.

"His cousin," I say.

"Fats Domino?" Mr. Hernandez leans on his desk. "How do you know about him?"

"Everybody knows him," Turi says. "Every time he's in town for a concert Mr. Blueberry Hill goes and gets his fix at Monchie's house."

Mr. Hernandez nods. "Sounds like you'd be a good reporter, Arturo."

Turi stops pacing. "Me? Yeah right, like the TV would hire someone like me."

"If you go to college and study," Mr. Hernandez says, "why not?"

"College? Yeah, I'll jump in my DeLorean with my best friend Chad Hartnell and we'll go to UTEP together."

Mr. Hernandez laughs out loud at that one. "Well, maybe not the DeLorean, but UTEP. I can see you at UTEP, and why couldn't you be friends with Chad?"

"You're funny, Mr. H." Turi starts pacing again.

"Mr. Hernandez, please."

"Isn't Chad like twenty-two years old and he's still playing foot-ball?" I say.

"Chad Hartnell is not that old." Mr. Hernandez sits on his desk.

"He's older than us, and we're in the same grade," Jimmy says. "I got a brother that played football with him."

"I think he was held back a year." Mr. Hernandez looks at us.

"Why? He's no dummy," Turi says.

"To get bigger." I raise my hands over my head.

"Bigger?" Turi puts both hands on a desk.

"Yeah, you know, for football." I pretend to throw him a pass.

"No way, that's messed up." Turi pretends to catch it and runs up the aisle a bit. "No one would hold their kid back in school unless they were dummies. No."

"You're right, Jennifer. Correct." Mr. Hernandez puts his hand up to ask for the ball. "How'd you know about that?"

"I thought everybody knew," I say. "Coach Hartnell tried to get me to play basketball on the girls' team and Chad's sister told me. She hates his guts."

"You play basket?" Mr. Hernandez pretends to catch the pass Turi has thrown.

"I did, when I was dumb." I clutch the sides of the desk in front of me.

"Why is that playing dumb?" He's waving a "go long" sign to Turi.

"It's not the playing. I liked playing. It's that I don't need another woman yelling at me to do stupid, pointless shit, stuff. That's what my mom does, and the coaches talked about us like we didn't know English or something, right there in front of us, saying how 'they' made the little Rebollo Mexican girl into the athlete and woman she is today. Like they even know what a woman is."

"Suzie Rebollo? The one who plays for UTEP now?" Mr. Her-nandez throws the ball, then rubs his chin.

"Yeah, Suzie. Her dad plays in the Mexican leagues. She took the bus from Juárez at four every morning to get here, and she got yelled at every morning for being late to practice. She hated it. What crazy person would want that?"

"I see your point, Jennifer, but look how it paid off for Suzie. I am guessing she's going to school, probably on a basketball scholarship. You could do that too."

"Nah, it's because she was smart. Her mom's a professor in Juárez. My dad just barely got out of high school, and my mom, I think she got her GED but maybe not. You went to college, right?"

"Where'd you live when you were here?" Jimmy asks.

"On the West Side," Mr. Hernandez says in a low voice.

"What did your dad do? I'll bet he didn't haul chickens like mine does." I grip the table edges harder.

"No, no, he didn't. He's a lawyer here in town."

"That's pretty cool. So he works with all the white people." Turi tosses the imaginary ball back to Mr. Hernandez. "My mom works for rich people."

"My dad owns his own business," Jimmy says.

Mr. Hernandez stops his throw midair. "That's great— what does he do?" He throws the ball to Jimmy.

"He's a plumber. Well, it's a septic service, but he does plumbing." Jimmy ignores the toss. "He does it on the side."

Turi runs behind Jimmy's desk and pretends to pick up the ball. "Why just on the side?"

"He doesn't have a license." Jimmy looks down.

"Why not? He can take the test, and he'll be bonded." Turi throws Mr. Hernandez the ball.

"Yeah, we know." Jimmy keeps looking at his desk.

"He from here?" I say.

"Yeah, he's American." Jimmy looks at me like he wants to fight. "We all are."

"Well then, he can own a business. That would be cool." I practically whisper.

"He does. A septic-system business. He does all right." Jimmy won't look up.

"But he could do better, no?" Turi catches another pass from Mr. Hernandez.

"Yeah, he could." Jimmy traces the names carved onto the desktop with his fingers.

"Does he not know where to go?" Turi holds the imaginary football in the air. "What's the problem?"

"Get off my back, will you?" Jimmy turns and puts both hands on the back of his chair and stares at Turi. He acts like he wants to get up, but something is holding him down.

"Hey, sorry," I say. "We don't mean nothing."

Jimmy turns and looks at his desk again, then after a long time says, "Not your fault. He doesn't read too good, that's all."

"How'd he get the septic-service business?" Mr. Hernandez sits on his desk again.

"You don't gotta take a test, just sign papers." Jimmy pretends to scribble. "He's a good plumber. He can fix anything."

"You know, school's not for everybody," Mr. Hernandez says. "Some people don't do well holed up in a room like this one for hours at a time. In college, they taught me that people have different ways of learning—some people have to *do* to learn."

"What you mean?" Jimmy says.

"Well, instead of reading in a book that four minus two equals two," Mr. Hernandez stands and pulls out his wallet, "you give that person four bucks and you tell them to give you two and then ask them what's left."

"There'd be nothing left if you gave me four bucks." Turi pretends to run. "I'd split out of here with the cash."

Jimmy laughs and nods his head.

"Those people learn by *doing* instead of listening." Mr. Hernandez puts his wallet back in his pocket. "It's called tactile learning. I'll bet you're dad is one of those people."

"Ah, yeah, that's exactly how my dad is. He can fix anything. A car, a clogged sink, a leaky roof, but he gets all nervous whenever I bring home my books from school."

"I'm the opposite of your dad." Mr. Hernandez rubs an open hand on his wide chest. "I get nervous whenever the mechanic pops open the hood of my car because I don't know what to do."

We all laugh.

"You can change the hell out of a light bulb." Jimmy smiles wide.

146

"That's the extent of my manual-labor knowledge." He points up to the light fixture with no bulb.

"You can lift heavy desks." I tap the top of my desk.

"Thank you, Jennifer, for the kind yet patronizing words." Mr. Hernandez smiles.

"Pat-ra who?" Turi asks.

"Patronizing," Mr. Hernandez says. "This is a good word for you guys to know, because this happens to you all the time, really to all teenagers. Teachers patronize you, principals, parents, TV station anchors—"

"Okay, okay, but what is it?" I wave my hand in the air.

"Patronizing is when people treat you like you're stupid." Mr. Hernandez walks to the chalkboard and grabs a piece of chalk and spells out P-A-T-R-O-N-I-Z-E. He points to the word. "When people think they know more than you do, so they simplify things for you and talk to you in a certain tone of voice."

"Cops, too. Cops do it a lot, too," Jimmy says.

"I'm the patrón of patronizing then," Turi hops on one leg. "All the teachers here talk to me like I'm a dumbass."

"You're not dumb, just an ass," I say.

"And you're a smartass." Turi smiles and throws the pretend football at me full force.

"I'm going tell Mrs. Delaney, 'Quit patronizing me,' whenever she talks to me all loud and slow like I'm deaf and stupid or some thing." Turi shakes his head.

"You should," Mr. Hernandez says. "She'll be surprised."

"Patronizing." I try the word out. I like it. I'm gonna tell my dad. He'll like it too. It's how Mom treats us.

Turi bends down like he's in a huddle. "So when do we start?"

Mr. Hernandez puts the chalk down on his desk and wipes his hands on his jeans. "What do you mean, Arturo?"

Turi makes like he's going to tackle Mr. Hernandez. "When we gonna learn something?"

I shake my head and would like to throw a real football at Turi's head. For the first time since I started, I think I'm going to like school.

Good Father

OPENING DAY IN Alamo City's freshly raked baseball field started with all the fanfare and cattiness of New York's fashion week. The tall, muscular, teenage Bobcat team infielders worked the crowd with their opening-day razzle-dazzle. Dalton Reyes pitched the first ball of the season and everyone cheered as Junior Hernandez caught it and then stretched his six-foot-two frame up out of its crouching position then made a sharp throw to second that echoed, like a slap across the face in an empty room, when the second baseman caught it. Second shot it to first, who threw the ball to third. The third baseman pitched it to shortstop, and the entire infield ran it into Dalton and Junior. Behind the backstop, Ernesto Hernandez watched with the pride of a former player who was used to being admired as the team gathered around his oldest son, Junior. He surveyed his younger son, Sergio, standing in the outfield with his teammates in his black-and-red uniform with his cap over his heart. He thought, even though his youngest wasn't going to have the height of his older brother, he would have the speed that the eluded the eldest. Both kids surpassed even his skills when he was their age.

Bobcat head coach Steven Springer met the team on the mound, where he took a microphone that was run out to him by the mayor's son. Ernesto shook his head. The young pony leaguer was given this privilege for his faithful attendance to every practice, but Ernesto and some others whispered that Adam was on the field because of Sam Butler's position in town. Coach Springer read the little league pledge of allegiance and called the Reverend Amit Gupta up to the mound to give a prayer. All the pomp and circumstance culminated with Sheila Jenkins singing "The Star-Spangled Banner." Her father, Chad, teared up every time she sang the song. Ernesto knew Chad was thinking of the friends he had lost in Desert Storm. The people in the crowd, made up of parents, grandparents, teenagers, and young children, commented to one another how Sheila sounded just like she did on television when she sang at Kyle Stadium at the Aggie/Longhorn Thanksgiving-day matchup. Although Sheila was quoted in *The Radio Dispatch* as saying she preferred larger crowds and the cold football weather to this warm spring day, the high school senior was happy to practice the national anthem one more time before singing the song in her triple-A debut in Round Rock the following week. The article took Ernesto back to his Mexican League days. After the crowd cheered, the president of the little league, Lee Greene, walked to mound and said, "Play ball!" The crowd cheered some more and then dispersed.

Ernesto followed the Mudcats to the farthest of four identical fields to watch them warm up. He stood a few feet away from the first-base dugout and rested his forearms over the chain link fence as the players stretched. He wondered why Coach Morgan wasn't walking them through these exercises. He couldn't understand why the team was so undisciplined. When Ernesto coached, he walked them through warm-up and made sure the team was thorough. These players were sloppy and slow about the whole affair. Ernesto rolled his eyes after seeing the coach in the dugout on his cell phone, and he worried that he had made a mistake by allowing Sergio to decide which team he would play for this spring. The Mudcats took the field when the umpire shouted that they should play ball. This jarred Coach Morgan away from his phone conversation, and he snapped his cell shut, then put it in his pocket. Joe Leopold ran past Ernesto wearing khaki pants with dress shoes and slipping a Mudcats' jersey over his Oxford shirt. The team skipped their infield warm-up because these men thought more of work than the game. Ernesto decided he would talk to them after the game—teach them a thing or two. By the second inning, Ernesto was gripping the chain link fence in anger because of the poor coaching.

He watched his son catch a line drive, then pitch it underhanded to the second baseman for what could have been a double play. Sergio moved the ball from his black glove to his hand in one continuous motion. He was as practiced and studied as his father was at work when he lined up his mower to a distant marker at the start of a run. But Sergio's feet were an inch off the dirt as he threw, and this made the toss high. Ernesto hooked his callused fingers into the chain link fence and shook it.

He yelled in Spanish, "What's wrong with you, Sergio? Think!"

Sergio kept his eyes on the sand in front of him but nodded his head.

Coach Morgan yelled, "Shake it off, Sergio, and be ready next time. It's coming to you."

Ernesto crossed his arms, rested them on his large, hard belly, and watched the next batter. He would have never put Chance Reyes on second base, he thought. The kid is too short. Chance should be playing third. He's quick and has a good arm. Between Sergio and Chance nothing could get through to left field. This team doesn't know how to work hard. If coached right, this team could go places.

Julie Reyes walked up to Ernesto and gave him an awkward sideways hug so their bellies wouldn't collide. She dropped the metal folding chair she carried and it shook the fence.

"Ernie, how are our boys doing?" she wheezed.

"They're ahead four to three with two outs in the second." Ernesto kept his eyes on the field as he spoke. "Sergio messed up a double play, but *Shance* brought a runner in with a pop fly to right field in the first inning."

"That's our boy!" Julie pumped her fist. "In the first game, too."

"Where's my compadre, Octavio?" Ernesto touched his ear, and Sergio backpedaled from the dirt onto the grass.

"Working," Julie said, watching her son and then Ernesto.

"Muevete," Ernesto sidestepped away from the coach to keep his line of sight clear. He grunted, then said, "Working a double shift?" He touched his ear again.

"You bet. With this one on the way, he's been pulling more and more of those." She pointed to her belly and watched Chance back up toward the grass, too.

"One more and you'll have an entire infield." Ernesto glanced at Julie for the first time. She pulled her long, blonde hair through the adjuster of the cap. He smiled when he read on her red-and-black jersey, "Baby Mudcat on Deck"; it had a picture of a baseball bat underneath, pointing to her belly.

"Yeah, yeah, that's what Tavie says." She rubbed her belly. "And you could coach them all."

"I would. But . . ." He bent down and unfolded the metal chair for Julie.

"I don't understand. Why aren't you coaching this year?" She stepped in front of the chair so that the coach standing outside the dugout couldn't overhear.

"They won't let me." He pointed behind him toward a green concession stand.

"What? You mean Chad and Lee don't want you coaching?" She eyed the green hut behind her as if they could hear her from that distance.

"I don't understand either." Ernesto clapped when Sergio caught a deep pop fly and the team ran into the dugout. "My team went to the playoffs last year. And still they don't let me coach."

"Nice job, Mudcats! Way to go, Serge!" Julie yelled and clapped. "You know about Chad and Lee, right?" she whispered.

"I know them—" He clapped. "Come on, Sergio, you've got this McGarrety. All his pitches are high and outside just the way you like them."

The coach stepped in Ernesto's line of sight and walked Sergio to the on-deck circle as he took his place near third base.

"Good, he's telling him to take the first two pitches because McGarrety starts out wild."

151

"How do you know?" Julie waved her hand in her face like a fan.

"Everybody knows." Ernesto nodded his head and turned to Julie, whose freckled face was pink. "He held up two fingers. What else could he be saying?"

Julie giggled.

"What about Chad and Lee?" He leaned a forearm on the fence in front of him to watch the game.

"I went to high school with them." Julie placed both hands on the fence to steady herself.

"Yes, and so did Octavio." He watched Sergio take the first pitch, which was high.

"Tavie was never at the parties like I was. Way to watch!" Julie yelled, as the second pitch sailed over the catcher's mitt and hit the backstop.

"Too bad there was nobody on base," Ernesto said.

"Chad and Lee are not very nice and . . ."

Sergio hit the third pitch shallow, to center field.

Ernesto cupped his hands like megaphones and yelled. "Run, m'ijo, run fast, you can get a double. Córrele, córrele." He rubbed his hands across his chest. "Why did he hold him at first base? He could have made it to second. Carter throws high when he's in a hurry."

"Coach Morgan played ball in high school. I think he knows what he's doing," Julie said.

"Yeah, he's never coached a championship team. I have." Ernesto shook his head. "I don't care if they're not nice. Some people say I'm not nice. Who needs nice?"

"They especially aren't nice to Mexicans, if you know what I mean." She patted her belly.

"Oh, you mean they're prejudiced?" He peered at the on-deck circle. "Come on, Randy, pop it to left field."

"Yeah, if you want to call it that. How many Mexicans do you see coaching Pony League teams?" With cap in hand, Julie pointed to the field. "I've always thought that, and I've told Tavie."

"What does Octavio say?" Ernesto crossed his arms.

"He says I'm a chee . . . chee . . . chee something, but he doesn't know them like I do."

Ernesto laughed, then leaned on the fence. "Chinolera. He should know; he works with them at the plant."

"Yeah, but I went to school with them. And they have always been and always will be," Julie said. "They were brutal to Sarah Contreras in high school."

"Sergio, you should have taken off the minute the pitcher winded up." Ernesto punched the fence before turning to Julie. "What do you mean?"

"They picked on her mercilessly." She clinched the fence. "They called her Sarah Colossal-ass."

"You talking about Miss Contreras, who lives on Travis Street?" He saw the ball hit the dirt in front of the catcher.

"The very one." Julie shook the fence. "Don't swing."

"I do her yard." He scratched his head. "You two are the same age?"

"No, she's two years younger than me."

"Ah, you're kidding." He turned and looked at Julie. "Colossal-ass? What does that mean?"

"Colossal, you know—massive, huge." She stretched her arms wide. "Oh, look, he got a piece of it."

Ernesto turned to watch Randy running toward first. "Tag up! Tag up, m'ijo!"

Julie cupped her mouth, "Go, go, go!"

"Why did he hit it to center? Sergio could have been tagged out." Ernesto shook his head.

"He swung late is all," Julie said. "Way to advance the runner, Randy!"

"They're right, you know." Ernesto kicked at the fence as the next batter, Gustavo, planted his feet inside the batter's box. "It is pretty big."

She frowned, then waved her hands in the air, as if trying to clear away a fly. "They're racist. Why else won't they let you coach? You're practically coaching from the sidelines." She took a deep breath and yelled, "Go Gus!"

"Gustavo. It's Gustavo."

"That's what I said. Gus. Gus. Isn't that what I said?" She put her hands on her hips.

"It's Gustavo, Julia." Ernesto smiled.

She shook her head. "Oh, you and Tavie."

"What about me and Octavio?"

"Oh, Ernie, what's the big deal?"

Ernesto cleared his throat. "It's the name our—"

"Come on, Ernie, Erne . . ." Julie cooed.

Ernesto laughed and pointed toward the field. "Gustavo is going to bunt. The coach should just let him hit. He knows what he's doing."

"Chance is up next. He wants more runners on the bases," Julie said.

"Yeah, you're probably right." He wiped sweat from his forehead with a finger. "I think it's because of last year. I had Adam Butler on my team, and he didn't start."

"Oh, really?" Julie said. "Chad, Lee, and Sam Butler go hunting in Colorado together every winter break."

"Yeah, I know. I like the kid, but everybody knows he's not a starter. Sam wanted me to start him. There was no way I was going to put Adam in. We were on a winning streak. Sam tried to tell me that his kid was as good as Rodriguez's and Placensio's kids, and I told him, 'Adam needs to practice more before he can start.'"

Julie put her hand over her mouth to hide her laughter.

"I say to him, 'If you would get your glove on and go outside, spend some time teaching him how to field and catch pop flies, it would help him.'" Ernesto pointed above Julie's head.

"You didn't tell him that?" Julie blinked rapidly. "No wonder you're not coaching. Chad, Lee, and Sam are in Rotary, on the chamber board, and they go to church together."

"Yes, I did. And he tells me his son does come to practice." Ernesto kicked the fence and surveyed the field—he saw Sergio on third base and Gustavo on first. "You know that's not enough, right?"

154

Julie nodded her head in disbelief.

"So I said again, 'Adam needs to practice more.'" He stood erect and pointed four fingers at Julie. "'If you want your son to be a good player, you need to be a good father and spend some time practicing with him.'"

"Chance's up? What did I miss? Did Gus bunt?"

"Gustavo laid the ball down the third-base line and beat the throw easy." Ernesto crossed his arms.

"Let's go, Chance. Hit it out of the park!" Julie clapped.

"You can't expect a kid to practice once or twice a week and then start." Ernesto hit the fence. "I think of the Rodriguez and Placensio kids and how often Gregorio and Estefan practice with them, and there was no way I was gonna start Adam."

"I can't believe you." Julie laughed and tried to watch her son.

"Take two, Chance. He's wild," Ernesto yelled. He turned to face Julie and blocked her view of home plate. "So Sam's face is red and he's standing so close to me that I can smell the pickle on his breath. And I have my hands across my chest like this with my catcher's mitt on."

Julie stared at Ernesto's bare hands.

He stepped so close to Julie that their round bellies touched. "He's real close, so I tap him on the face with it."

"You hit him?" Her eyes widened.

"No." He shook his head. "I tapped him on the face, like this."

"Ouch!" Julie took an unbalanced step back and sat down in her lawn chair.

"You're all right." Ernesto crouched on one knee. "He was standing too close and I just gave him a little tap to back him up, like you just did. You know how tall he is, and he was standing over me. I'm not gonna let anybody get up in my face. I told him I'd do it again if he didn't back up."

Julie was silent.

The crowd in the stands yelled. "Go, Chance! Home run! Home run! Run, Chance!"

Julie peered at Ernesto out of the corner of her eye. She whispered, "I think it's a home run."

"No, it's a triplo." Ernesto leaned a hand on the chain link. "If Chance were a little bit faster he'd make it. Ruben's arm can snag even Gustavo from center field."

"Oh, what do you know?" She rubbed her cheek and watched the left fielder make a perfect throw to the catcher as Chance rounded third.

She's Got Game

BRANDY DIDN'T MIND when her brother, Eddie, tied her hand behind her back. He had his own way of looking at things, getting results. It was his friend, Adrian, she minded. His fat-lipped mouth never stopped flapping, and he always picked this time after school to drop by to play basket. Eddie's way of seeing made her tolerate Adrian's big-mouthed interruptions. The guy might even be cute if he weren't such a blabbermouth.

"You have to get it up out of your face, otherwise you won't be able to see what you're doing." Eddie held up a dirty shoelace.

"No way am I wearing a ponytail, never. Here in the front yard where everybody can see me." Brandy slapped at the lace in his hand. She had her own way of doing things too.

He wound the strip around his finger and nodded at something behind Brandy as he said, "You could cut your hair short—"

"Yeah, then your transformation would be complete." Adrian kicked gravel from the yard at her feet and onto the driveway.

"Transformation?" Brandy turned, fists clenched.

"You'll be a full-fledged dyke," Adrian laughed.

Before he closed his mouth, Brandy tried to press her knuckles in it.

"Would you two stop it? Stop it." Eddie pushed his little sister so hard she fell partly on the rocks and on the cement driveway.

He didn't touch Adrian. "This isn't going to get you a starting position on the Scorpions. You want to start, don't you?"

Brandy rolled onto her feet because the desert heat made the ground intolerable. "I really don't care."

"That's not true." Eddie looked up at her with his hands on his hips. "If I had your height, I'd be unstoppable. Sitting the bench sucks."

"Try managing." Adrian rubbed his mouth. "Now that sucks."

"Shut up," Eddie and Brandy said together and smiled.

Eddie looked at Adrian, then frowned. "Well, yeah, I guess you're right."

He was too soft on Adrian. Brandy thought he was too soft on every living thing. He was like their mother. The more pathetic the person, the nicer Eddie would be to them. Instead of hating their mother for her hanging out at Rocky's Bar all the time, looking for a hookup, Eddie made excuses for her drinking and whoring. Brandy knew Eddie just felt sorry for her because Dad had beat her up so bad before he left for good. She deserved it. Brandy had lost count of how many "uncles" she was supposed to be nice to. Eddie said, "She was lonely and it was hard raising kids by herself." Brandy said, "It's hard on *us* raising *her* by ourselves." This usually made Eddie laugh. To Brandy, his laughter was like rain in the middle of the summer, and just as rare. Anyone who experienced it came away feeling hopeful and good. When she heard it, she could tolerate anyone Eddie was trying to rehabilitate, even Adrian.

She stepped toward Adrian, and he jumped back like he'd seen a rattlesnake. "Would you come on already? I wanna go inside and watch TV. Let's find the damn ball and let me shoot free throws, ya."

"Where's the rope?" Eddie searched the side of the house.

"Can't I just keep my hand behind my back this time?" Brandy stood under the basketball hoop.

"You could if you'd keep it there, but you don't. Right around ten shots—aha, here it is—your left hand starts creeping over. It messes with the arch on the ball." Eddie picked up the basketball he spotted. He tossed it in the air and blew on his hands. The smooth ball soaked up the one-hundred-degree heat like a sponge. He bounced it and blew while walking toward Brandy.

"Found it." Adrian pulled an orange nylon rope out of the Azalea bush, and its petals dusted the gray rocks pink.

Brandy sighed when she saw Adrian had found it and was snapping it in the air. She willed the rope to smack her brother.

Eddie tried to grab the end of the line that Adrian whipped. "Ouch, fucker. That hurt."

"I'm sorry." Adrian kept popping the rope.

Brandy felt guilty like she had hurt her brother. "This isn't a rodeo. Give it to him already."

"Stop it." Eddie threw the ball at him, which cut short Adrian's lassoing. "We need to do this before Oscar knows we're out here."

Oscar was the only person Eddie couldn't help. He was all muscle and anger. Oscar thought he was a real cowboy with the BB gun his real dad gave him. Before he left, Oscar's dad told him that a Border Patrol agent's son should have a gun. And like the migra, Oscar used it on Mexicans every chance he got.

"God, I hate that guy. It must suck to live next door to such an asshole. All right. All right." Adrian let the cord dangle. "Hey, let me tie her up, yah?"

"I'm going inside if he comes near me." Brandy lifted her hair and fanned her sweat-drenched neck.

Eddie held out his hand. "Give me the rope."

After of few minutes of intense staring, Adrian handed the rope to Eddie.

He was all business. "All right, Brandy, arm in."

She put her left arm behind her and raised her right as Eddie wrapped the orange cord around her ribs. She held one end with her left hand near the middle of her back as Eddie circled her six times, then met up with her end and tied the two pieces into a large bow.

"There. Done. Get to the mark." Eddie pointed to the ground. "Pass her the ball."

Adrian picked up the ball and threw it at Brandy as hard as he could. It hit her stomach. She doubled over for a few seconds, then looked up. Red faced, she ran after him, and Adrian bolted into the street. Even one armed, she knew she could take him.

"Jesus, why the hell do you let that idiot come over?"

"Ah, Adrian's all right." Eddie picked up the basketball.

"You feel sorry for him, don't you? A sorry sack of—"

"His dad's all fucked up."

"I'd like to fuck him up." Brandy peered at Adrian across the street. "What? Like no arms or legs? Brain tumor?"

Eddie's eyes were sad. "Even with your temper, you can't do anything worse than his dad has."

"Oh, that kind . . ."

Eddie nodded, and his black eyes went to that place not even Brandy's basketball skills could bring him out of. There was silence as they both watched Adrian in the middle of street.

"You think Mom's coming home tonight?" Brandy asked.

"Nah, it's Thursday, Ladies' Night." Eddie picked up the basketball.

"Half-price drinks—cheap loser night. She'll love it."

"Quit it." Eddie raised his voice and bounced the ball to her.

"You're right." Brandy dribbled. "She's at the library." Bounce. "Meeting a doctor." Bounce. "He has a cure for drinking." Bounce. "They're drinking coffee." Bounce. "Talking about marriage." Bounce. "We're moving to the West Side."

Eddie stole the ball from her and laughed. The cement sparkled its heat dance.

"What's your problem?" Adrian yelled. He picked up a rock and threw it. It landed between Brandy and Eddie.

"Let's get this over with already," Brandy said. Her free hand was up.

Eddie bounced her the ball. "Yeah, you gotta finish before Oscar gets home. If he sees you like this, he'll—"

She shot a free throw and it went in the metal hoop.

"You're too close. You gotta back up to the second oil stain." Eddie pointed to the oil-stained cement drive as he shagged the ball.

"No, it's the first," Brandy said.

"No, it's the second. Remember, I measured it." He walked under the hoop and took two giant steps toward the stain.

"Yah, you measured, but I'm the one that got in trouble for cutting up the stalk in Mrs. Carter's yard." Brandy patted her chest. "Where's the lechuguilla? I'll show you. We marked it. I was there."

"Yeah, well so was Adrian," he said. "But the yardstick got mulched."

"After all I went through?" Brandy pointed to the street. "Ask him then."

Eddie cupped his hands and yelled, "Where's the free-throw line?"

"Second stain, fool. You should remember, you measured," he yelled back.

"See, I told you." Eddie pushed the ball into Brandy's stomach.

"All right." She took two steps backward and shot a free throw. Then she said, "Two"

"No, that's one. The other one didn't count." Eddie rebounded.

"Does it really matter?" She held up her hand for the ball.

"Yes, of course it matters. You want to be the best player on the team, don't you? You want to beat the crap out of all the other players, no? You want to be the one everyone talks about at school? You want to be in the paper?" He held the ball to his side.

Brandy looked in her brother's intense eyes. She didn't have the heart to say no. She knew how hard he worked and how he always came up short. She said, "One."

"That's what I thought," he bounced the ball to her. "You're going to get the best-athlete award your sophomore year, if it kills me."

"You're insane." She shook her head and the sweat from the tips of her hair that sprinkled the cement disappeared the second it landed. She shot and missed. "Crap. Do I really have to start over?"

"Not insane, just committed." Eddie clapped his hands. "How else are you going to learn? If I let you slide, then you'll miss these shots in the big game."

From across the street, Adrian yelled, "Faggot."

Eddied looked over at him and then at Brandy, who was about to shoot another free throw. "You know, he's right."

"What? That you're a faggot." Brandy chuckled.

"No, stupid. You need to flick your wrist." Eddie said. "If you flick your wrist, you'll get a good arch on the ball. Gimme the ball. Look." He sank three shots in a row. "It's in every time."

"Oh, okay. Let me try." Brandy put up her palm to get the ball. She caught it and balanced it in her one free hand.

Adrian yelled, "Run! He's got the gun."

Brandy and Eddie heard gravel crunch and their neighbor Oscar's deep voice. "That's what all of you are—a bunch of faggots."

Eddie and Brandy backed up. She was trying to squirm out of the rope while keeping an eye on the slender rifle at Oscar's side. Eddie undid the bow he made and the orange rope fell to the ground. He touched Brandy's elbow and they both took off in separate directions. It was a practiced move. Brandy knew she was the target. Oscar liked her. She felt the first sting in her calf. She heard the pump of the air rifle, then felt the second prick in the small of her back. She yelped in pain. "You suck!" She hated to think what he would do to her if he didn't have a crush on her.

"You wish, faggot," he yelled as he kept shooting and missing.

Brandy cleared a rock wall in seconds. Behind the barrier she examined her wounds. She saw a mosquito bite–sized welt form on her calf and her back was sore. When she realized Oscar hadn't followed her, she peeked over the fence and saw a white glitter rock coming at her face. She ducked and the rock landed in the dirt behind her. She picked it up and cocked her arm.

"You all right, Brandy?" She heard Eddie from somewhere over the fence. "He's out of ammo. Run!"

Brandy popped up, scaled the fence, and saw Oscar halfway hidden behind a trash can, trying to reload. The steel balls spilled out onto the rocks. She aimed, then chucked the white glitter rock at his head. He ducked. The rock hit the trash can, ricocheted, and got him in the face. She laughed and ran fast before he finished reloading.

"Inside! Inside!" Adrian and Eddie screamed while holding the door open.

Brandy slid through the open door across the linoleum floor like a runner sliding into home.

Adrian waved his arms like an umpire. "You're safe."

Eddie slammed the door shut.

"Jesus Christ, I should just dance with Ceci and Karen in their garage," Brandy said, out of breath, to the ceiling.

"You'd kill yourself in ten minutes if you hung out with them, and you'd never make all-district." Eddie's breath was almost even. He looked down at her and gave her his hand.

"Yeah, you're probably right." She slapped it away, breathing hard.

"Why does he hate you so much?" Adrian held his stomach as he crouched against the door.

"I dunno," she mumbled.

Adrian inhaled like he was about to go underwater, then let it out. "Yeah, you do."

"You think I'm telling you anything? Right." Brandy brushed her hair out of her face but stayed on the cool floor.

"I gotta go." Eddie jumped over Brandy and headed for the bathroom.

Adrian hopped up. He waited until the door shut to pounce on Brandy. He sat on her stomach and grinded his knees into her arms. "Why does Oscar always go after you?"

She didn't struggle.

"Why, Brandy? You got a secret?"

Her arms hurt, and she thought of shoving him off, but she had never been this close to Adrian. His dark-brown eyes had flecks of beige in them as if dust storms were blowing right inside him. She wondered if this was what it was like to be hypnotized. "We kissed once."

"What?" He looked down at her and pushed his knees down harder. "You kissed *him*?"

Brandy sucked air and her chest heaved. "It wasn't a bad idea at the time."

"Ugh, him? That's, that's gross." Adrian looked up toward the bathroom door. "Does Eddie know?"

There was silence. The hum of the swamp cooler seemed deafening. When she heard the sound of water running, she looked toward the restroom door and then up at Adrian. Adrian looked better when he didn't talk. His lips were inches away from hers. He dug his knees into her arms, then licked the corner of her mouth. Her eyes grew wide. She didn't move. He lifted some of his weight off of her arms and licked her again, but this time she opened her mouth a bit. His tongue went inside and they were both surprised. The sound of the door opening seemed to wake Brandy and she pushed Adrian off. He fell backward and hit his head on the wall. He moved toward her, and although she didn't want to she spun around and kicked at him. He laughed but kept coming. When Eddie appeared, Brandy's foot caught Adrian's jaw. He held his wounded face between his legs.

Eddie put his hands on his hips. He looked like he did after a basketball game when he rode the bench. "Would you stop picking on Adrian? One of these days he's going to get you—good."

Duck, Duck, Goosed

EVERY TIME JIM BURKETT caressed Anita Guerra's arm she had to suppress her desire to flinch. She wondered if the red dress or the low neckline was giving Jim the wrong impression. Anita felt his bony fingers on her shoulder. After Jim laughed at his own joke, pistonlike, those fingers felt their way down her bare arm to her elbow.

"I hear they're letting the Mexican Baptist church sell tamales at the fair this year." Jim held her arm at the joint. "I'll bet you make some good tamales, don't you, Anita?"

"Well, no, I've never made them." Anita took a sip from her red plastic cup and Jim's grip slipped. "We usually buy them from the Hernandez brothers like everybody else."

Jim closed his eyes and patted the wool Texas Rangers cap he wore like he was stroking one of his retrievers. "You know what some of my favorite foods are?"

She ticked off a list of bland food she'd seen his wife bring to garden-club meetings: casserole, ambrosia salad, pimento cheese sandwiches, tuna fish salad. Then she scanned the room looking for Craig.

"I love that Spanish rice. Really love that rice and beans. Anita, I'll bet you make that rice real spicy for Craig. Don't you?" Spit from Jim's mouth landed on Anita's cup. "I eat at La Mexicana every day because of that Spanish rice."

"Actually, we eat mainly meatloaf or spaghetti at home."
Anita frowned, feeling embarrassed. "Because of the kids."

"You don't say?" Jim tipped the bill of his cap. "Kids change
everything, don't they? Your girls are beautiful. They've got your
skin color."

"Ah, thank you." Anita looked down at the rim of her cup
where the spit had landed. She didn't drink from it. If Jim had
attended her high school in Del Rio, he would have been one of
the boys who picked on her because she was so dark, she
thought.

She was relieved that Jim's grip was no longer on her. She
didn't like anyone touching her in public, besides her husband;
even that degree of intimacy took Craig years of negotiating.
Still, she didn't get much time to talk with adults and was glad
to be out of the house. Despite Jim's molestation, the second
vodka tonic was going down easy and she was feeling good.

"Excuse me." Mela Burkett crept up from behind Anita, took
her other arm, then pressed her large, cushy chest against it.
"They're beautiful, just like their mother."

Mela's teeth reminded Anita of the shiny lug nuts that were
perfectly aligned on the windowsills in Craig's shop. She always
felt the urge to knock them out of place; instead she would
straighten them. She remembered telling Craig that all four of
the Burkett children were entitled just like him, after Jim pro-
tested an umpire's call on the softball field from the stands. As
usual, Craig ignored her then laughed and focused his attention
on his business. He had said, "I should have made Goodwin's
Body Shop bigger on their uniforms. I can barely read my name
from the stands."

Mela swiped a stray hair away from Anita's face, like a mother
would, so naturally. Anita smiled and stepped backward, away
from Mela's touch and right into David Phillips. His doughy
body was more forgiving than his cologne. She hadn't heard him
lurking there, and she inhaled the cloud that followed him.
Despite the Drakkar cologne, David couldn't get rid of the musky
sewer smell his skin soaked up from the treatment plant. He

held his red plastic cup so tight it pinched in the middle, and he drank from it like he needed to quench a thirst.

"Excuse me, honey." David touched Anita's bare back before stepping into the threesome.

Anita straightened as David stood next to Mela and hung a soft arm around her shoulder.

"What are you all planning?" He shook Mela with the arm on her shoulder.

"Wouldn't you like to know?" Mela bumped his side with her fleshy hip. "You smell good, like always."

"Thank you, Sweetie." David smiled wide.

Anita, sandwiched between Mela and Jim, thought about how glad she was to be out of the house and talking with adults.

"Jim was just explaining to Anita, here," Mela's glossy, red fingernails zipped through the air as she pointed from one person to another, "how much he looooves eating at La Mexicana."

"I know. I know. Spanish rice." David slid his arm off Mela's shoulder and dropped it down to her side. His hand disappeared in her hip where he held and pulled Jim's wife in close. "You'd think it was King Casserole from Betty's Diner or Mela's dumplings the way he goes on and on about it. I think it's the scenery he likes."

Mela squeezed David's hand at her hip. "Well, those waitresses sure are pretty, just like Anita."

"They sure are." Jim tried to slap Mela's back from behind Anita. He missed, and his arm brushed against Anita's backside. "Shoot, I'd love for Mela to cook up rice and beans every once and a while. She can't cook anything besides dumplings."

Anita felt her face get hot. She smiled and thought about being cooped up all day with three little girls, and how good it felt to slip on her black pumps.

Jim hung a wiry arm around Anita's shoulder and wondered if he mistook her smile as an invitation.

"Oh, quiet, you old coot. You'll eat anything that's set in front of you," Mela said.

David and Jim both chuckled.

"Would you two change the subject already? Your dirty minds are gonna run Anita off." Mela pointed at Anita.

"Where do you put it? You eat as much as your horses and you're as a skinny as a bean pole." David patted his large belly with his free hand. "I need some of what you've got."

"You've already had it." Jim rubbed circles over his crisp Cinch button-down and squeezed Anita's shoulder with his other hand. His large diamond-studded Aggie ring caught on the fourth button down, where his rock-ribbed belly began, and stopped his motion. "I do love to eat. You're right. You're right. I eat it all."

David cracked up, and the force of his laughter shook Mela.

"I wonder where Craig ran off to." Anita scanned the Knights of Columbus Hall.

"Would you two change the subject already? I'm bored." Mela stood ramrod straight.

"You'd be bored if you were talking to the Lee Greenwood himself," Jim said. "You all ever been to the Mexican swap meet here on the first Thursday of the month?"

"I don't know how they do it, but they transform this shed into little Mexico." David spread his free hand out in front him. "Booths, a live band with a tuba player, Christmas lights hanging from the wall, and paper deals hanging from the ceiling, and the smells, oh, the smell of barbeque, hot sauce, and lime."

"How do they get anything to stick to these metal walls?" Mela said. "If it's cold sometimes even duct tape won't hold, and when it's hot Mr. Arce won't let us use duct tape."

Everyone scanned the bare aluminized-steel walls.

"Near impossible to get off," Jim said and squeezed Anita.

"They probably use electrical tape. It comes in great colors." Anita tried to step out from under Jim's arm but he followed her.

"Speaking of, Rudy Jimenez came into the dealership on a Friday afternoon and brought five thousand dollars in cash in dollar bills," Jim said. "No lie."

"Where does a guy like that get that kind of money?" David looked at Anita.

Anita wiped the rim of her cup before taking a sip and thought about telling Jim the proper way to pronounce Rudy's last name, but she decided this battle wasn't worth the fight. Her weakness angered her.

"Anita, honey? You okay?" Mela touched her other shoulder.

"What? Yes, yes, Rudy told me he's been waiting tables since before I was born. He did it in Mexico and just kept on when he got to Alamo City." Anita took a large swallow from her cup.

"Don't that beat all?" David pinched Mela's side.

"Oh, you're such a flirt!" Mela bumped him again.

"I'm not just a flirt; I can deliver, too." He looked at Anita and winked.

Anita blushed and scanned the room for Craig. He was waving his hands in the air, explaining something to Father Chacko. She could tell by the exaggerated gestures that he was drunk. When Craig noticed her staring at him, he blew a kiss at her. She knew he was having a good time. She decided she would too, so she peered across the room, looking for another way out of the conversation. She spotted Less and Geneva Donavan, who were undoubtedly talking about the county fair with the Fritzes. Anita found herself wondering what big name was coming to town to perform at this year's fair.

"Do you all know who's coming to the fair this year?" Anita looked at Mela.

"I heard it was Mark Chesney," she said.

"Who's that?" Anita gulped her drink.

"Some up-and-comer," David said. "It's Kenny."

"It's amazing how this town always gets these groups before their star rises." Mela flashed her nails into the air.

"We're a good-luck town." Jim pulled Anita in for a squeeze just as she was about to drink. She spilled some of the liquid, which stopped him short.

"I'm sorry about that," Jim said.

"We've had Randy Travis, Aaron Watson, and Pat Green before they got so big," David told Mela. "Randy Travis even had a few drinks with us. He's a hell of a guy."

"I do like a tall drink of water," Mela cooed, and she smothered her large, boxy body into David's pudgy one. "But mostly it's men that I like. Mostly."

Craig nudged between Anita and Mela and Jim took his arm off Anita. Anita exhaled as if she'd been holding her breath all these minutes. She touched Craig's hand. Before Craig could turn to look at her, Mela grabbed his arm and snuggled in close. Her breasts distracted him as she rubbed them against his rib cage.

Anita flashed hot when she noticed that Craig didn't move away.

Red faced, Craig said, "I was explaining to the chaplain, err, Father, that a hundred wooden crosses with pictures of fetuses on the church courtyard along Main Street isn't good for economic development."

Anita nodded her head. The church courtyard *was* an eyesore. Father Chacko was proud of the attention he had gotten for the Catholic Church when he and his congregation erected the abortion monument. There was no way he would take it down.

"Oh, honey, those Catholics are a gloomy bunch," Mela said. "That's why we're Methodist."

"Yes, yes, it's Catholicism lite, with less guilt, less filling." David let Mela go.

"Now, I don't know about you all, but the Catholic Church seems to be doing something right." Jim spread his palms open. "They're busting at the seams with young people."

"It's all those Spanish people that are coming into town." Mela squeezed Craig's arm.

"There are no Spaniards in Alamo City, Mela." Craig shook his head. "It's Mexicans you're thinking of."

"Oh, don't say that, that's just awful," Mela whispered. She caressed his arm.

"What?" Craig looked at Anita. "Mexican? What's so bad about saying Mexican?"

Mela continued to whisper and caress. "They don't like to be called that, do they, Anita?"

Anita looked at Mela's hand motions for what like seemed

hours. The conversation seemed to be slipping away from her. She knew she should talk, respond, but if she opened her mouth without getting her emotions under control she would scream, then they would talk about the spicy Mexican woman Craig had married, how emotional and volatile a culture, and she'd be more of a caricature than she already was. She wondered why the Burketts were such a touchy-feely couple. The things everyone said dumbfounded her, and her response to the question was to look down her nose at Mela.

Craig touched her elbow. "Nita?"

"I think it's only bad if you say it the wrong way." She hated how she sounded, complicit.

"What Anita is trying to say is that there is nothing wrong with calling someone Mexican." Craig said. "I mean, that is what those people are. Anita's grandparents are Mexican, and she uses the word all the time to describe them."

Anita hated herself for not being able to explain. She hated Craig for explaining as if he were an expert, no, *the* expert on Mexican culture. Yet she was grateful. She was thankful that he was there talking for her, otherwise, who would explain? She couldn't find the words, and he could. In fact, he always found the right words and used them, revved them up like a hot rod and spat them out at her like a teenager showing off his new car's muscle at a stoplight. He was especially accelerated when asking for sex. Craig wanted the hot and spicy Mexican beauty of his fantasies in bed, but all she could offer him was meatloaf and he was always disappointed. She wiped the rim of the cup and took another big sip of her vodka tonic.

"Can I get you another drink, señorita?" Jim asked Anita.

Feeling weighed down, she nodded and held her cup tight.

Mela said, "Craig, can I ask you about that private school you're sending your daughters to?"

Anita's mood lifted at the mention of her children. One thing she got right in Craig's eyes.

"Ah, sure." Craig looked nervous.

Anita sensed his tension. Everyone in his hometown was

upset with him for sending his kids up the road to Johnson City for school. At garden club, she'd overheard Geneva talking with Kay about how Craig didn't think the elementary school in Alamo City was good enough for his children. Yet, it was good enough for Craig. They found it strange that after coming back from the big city things had changed. Anita knew *big city* and *change* really meant Craig's wife. Craig hadn't changed. He was still the liberal, loudmouthed, wrongheaded kid everyone put up with, but Anita felt intruded upon every minute of the day. It seemed as though people in the town forced her to explain every decision she had made in life. Craig also intruded and misunderstood her. His exoticized fantasies of dark women fueled an appetite in him that she couldn't keep up with. She wouldn't keep up with. Even something as simple as registering the girls for private school was a minefield for Anita. Rosemary, the school's secretary, who went to school with Craig, took it upon herself to fill out their paperwork herself.

When Anita had asked to see it and changed her last name from Goodwin to Guerra, Rosemary said, "You are married, right?"

"Yes," Anita said.

"So your name is Anita Goodwin."

"No, my name is Anita Guerra," Anita laughed.

"But you're married." Rosemary tilted her head.

"Yes. I kept my name."

"You what?" she squinted.

"I kept it. My name." Anita pointed to herself.

"Why?" Rosemary shook her head.

"Because I like it." Anita exhaled.

"But you're married," Rosemary said with clinched fists.

Anita realized that her sarcasm was wasted and decided on a different tactic. "I'm one of those annoying feminists," she said.

Rosemary had nodded as if she had finally understood.

Rosemary, like everyone in Alamo City, found Anita baffling. Most confusing of all was that Craig brought her home. They all figured that Craig thought he was better than everybody else. "And sometimes he is," Anita thought and sipped her drink.

Mela was close enough to kiss Craig. "Is it worth the extra money you been paying per month, honey?"

"Oh, sure," he said as he tried to step away from her, but she clung tight. "They're heavy on schoolwork. Athletics comes second. Still, physical activity is important."

"Do you mind me asking: How much do you pay? We're thinking about sending Cody. He's been getting into a lot trouble lately, especially with a certain Jimenez girl." Mela looked at Anita. "She seems to have some kind of hold on him."

Anita laughed too loud. "Teenagers."

"Well, it's close to seven hundred a month," Craig said.

Mela whistled loud. "I didn't realize that the price of education was the same as a mortgage, if that don't beat all. You'd need to fix ten cars a week to keep up with those payments."

Through clenched teeth Craig said, "The price of a child's education is worth every penny."

Craig glanced at Anita. She knew it hurt him to say that. It served him right. It was the same line she'd use on him when he'd start up. Craig complained about the private school payment every month when he paid the bills. She was the one who had insisted on the private school. She couldn't imagine sending the girls to school with the Burkett or Phillips kids. Now he was using her words to defend himself. Don't that beat all? she thought.

"What's so funny, señorita?" Jim returned with her drink.

She took the full drink, nested it into her empty cup, gulped it, and frowned.

"What's wrong with it?" Jim pointed. "Gin and tonic, right?"

"I prefer vodka." Anita hoped he would leave again.

"Well, drink that one up then I'll get you one you like. It'll do the same job." Jim smiled and buffed his fingers against her side.

Before she could answer or move away from him, the pastor of the Methodist Church walked into the tight circle and it widened.

Richard Watson said, "I see you all are having a pastor-parish relations meeting. Shall I leave?"

"No." Anita grabbed his arm like it was a life ring.

173

Everyone laughed, then Ronnie Barton called the meeting to order.

Before they sat down, Craig gave her a look that said, "I know what I said, and I don't want to hear a word about it."

Anita gave him a tight-lipped smile. He frowned. She was feeling light-headed from the alcohol. She couldn't wait for the Pledge of Allegiance to end so she could dig into her barbecue ribs, mashed potatoes, and fried okra. She had to wait for the Rotary Pledge, the Passing of the Torch, and the dinner prayer before she was able to sit down to enjoy her meal. The dinner catered by the Big Bone Lick lived up to its namesake. The Rotary meeting was the same as last year's.

After dinner, when it came time to leave, the newly installed Rotary president Ronnie Barton hitched up his jeans before he bent low between Anita's and Craig's chairs and asked if they would like to stay late and help clean up, maybe have a few drinks afterward. Anita, who sat next to Pastor Watson and across from the Fritzes and Donavans, was having a good time. She didn't want the night to end, because that meant going home and dealing with Craig and the girls. She told Craig she wanted to stay.

"Are you sure?" Craig said.

"Yes, I'm having a good time. Just call Jason and tell him we'll be an hour late." Anita ignored his raised eyebrows. She tapped Geneva on the arm. "Like I was saying, I think it's a great idea to have Little Joe headline the fair one year."

Craig got up and followed Ronnie. Anita saw Craig place his car keys into an empty plastic ice cream container by the door that Ronnie pointed to. Anita was wondering how many people in the room Jason's father, Sheriff Welko, had given DWIs, then noticed that no one else at the table was invited to stay.

After everyone left, Anita and Craig helped throw trash away and put up tables. Anita drank beer from a can as they cleaned, and Craig kept bringing them to her.

"Would you stop bringing me these?" Anita swallowed.

"I'm not forcing you. Stop drinking them." Craig smirked and raised his eyebrows.

"I'm not like your ex." Anita saw that she had wiped the dirty thoughts from his head and the smile from his face, then added, "Alcohol isn't my aphrodisiac."

"Jesus, don't I know it. You're the only woman I know who likes to clean when she's drunk." Craig emptied plates into the trash can.

"You're lucky I'm drinking; otherwise the Knights of Columbus would charge the Rotary extra." Anita tugged the neckline of her dress over her breast.

"I'm your husband. I've seen your cleavage," Craig said, sliding a large green trash can to the table. "Not lately."

"We're in public." Anita flung a plastic cup in the trash. "I don't want everyone seeing it."

"God forbid you were sexual." Craig pitched plastic plates inside the container.

"What is that supposed to mean?" Anita stood straight.

"Nothing." Craig fired more trash into the can.

"A little help," Ronnie called out.

Craig left Anita and jogged across the cement floor to the other side of the room to help Ronnie drag an ice cooler filled with bottled beer across the cement floor to a group of chairs near the doorway. Both men heaved it onto one of the eleven fold-out chairs that were left out. David was arranging the chairs into a circle around Mela, who was already seated and drinking directly from a bourbon bottle. She had all the liquor bottles on the floor at her feet.

"S'cuse us, señorita, we've got to put this table away." Jim tipped his cap at Anita.

Anita backed away from the last table and headed toward the ring of seats near the doorway. Anita thought how small the room seemed without any tables, booths, lights, or decorations. The only color in the room was the American and Texas flags on freestanding poles framing the doorway. She watched Craig, who stood with Ronnie near the ice chest. He was congratulating Ronnie when she inhaled his smell—sharp lavender tinged with rotten egg.

"Sit, sit down, will ya? Make yourself comfortable, Sweetie," David patted the metal chair next to him.

Anita sat. She was tired of standing on heels and was happy for the opportunity to distract herself. She stopped pulling at the neckline of her dress. She sat up tall and pushed her chest out, then slouched, thinking that the V neck was cut too low.

"I won't bite," he said.

"Unless he's hungry," Joyce said, then sat down next to her husband with a sigh.

Kay Barton sat too but left a space for Ronnie between her and Joyce.

David ignored his wife.

"What are you thinking about, Anita?" David patted her knee. "You sure don't talk much."

"Just thinking." Anita stared across the intimate circle at Mela, who was still drinking the Wild Turkey from the bottle.

"About how handsome I am?"

"Ah, well, ah . . ." Anita remembered Mela saying at garden club that David liked his women "large and in charge." She looked at Joyce's petite frame and wondered if Mela was a size 24 or 26. "A child's game."

"Would you stop ribbing her, already?" Mela laughed. "This guy. When he's drunk, you better watch out."

"When I'm drunk? What about when you're drunk, Honey?" He looked to Joyce for confirmation.

"Watch out," Joyce said.

"You remember when we went skiing in Aspen?" David said.

"I don't recall anyone ever leaving the cabin," Mela cackled. "You were so drunk we threw you in the tub naked."

"And still that didn't sober you up," Joyce said.

"As I recall, I wasn't in that tub alone. She was pretty drunk too." David spread his legs wide as he nodded at Mela.

"That Coors enema took it out of me and Sheriff Welko too. Besides, someone had to take care of you," Mela said.

"What?" Anita said, then David's hand distracted her.

176

He patted Anita's knee. "I do like to be taken care of. I'll bet you take good care of your husband."

Anita sat frozen. She needed a drink. "Duck, Duck, Goose. That's the name of it."

"I'd like to goose you," David squeezed her knee.

"Wow, look at her. She's a beaut," Kay said as she sat across the circle from Anita. "Honey, stop coming on so strong. She doesn't need a country hick talking about getting taken care of and goosing. Have a bit more sophistication."

"Here, Sweetie, have some vodka. It's vodka you like, right?" Mela stood up and handed her a gallon jug of Smirnoff that was near her chair.

Anita accepted it gratefully. She set it on top of David's hand, which was on her knee, and held it tight. Her thoughts raced from enemas to Aspen to her childhood game of Duck, Duck, Goose. She remembered how as a girl her skull tingled when she was chosen. She hated the game because she never caught the person who chose her. She was always too slow.

David didn't move his hand. "Go ahead and drink it, Sweetie."

"Do you have a glass?" Her racing steps, frantic and clumsy, were foremost on her mind.

"We can find you one," Joyce said.

Kay leaned behind her to get Ronnie, Craig, and Jim's attention, "Honey, this sweetie wants a glass for her vodka."

"What for?" Jim looked their way. "She's got the bottle."

"I, ah, I don't like to drink from the bottle," Anita said.

Everyone laughed.

Craig caught Anita's eye and his brows furrowed. She pretended to be in on the joke and laughed with everyone.

"I'll get it. I'll get it." Anita stood, ridding herself of David's hand just as Jim walked up to her with a small, clear plastic cup.

"Here you go, Sweetie. Gimme the bottle and I'll pour you a drink." Jim filled her plastic cup to the rim with vodka.

"That's too much, too much." Anita spilled some of the drink

"That's what she said." Jim laughed loud and hard.

Craig was at her side. He tried to take the drink from her and she moved it away, spilling it on his new loafers.

"We need to get home, now," he said. "We should check on the girls. They're with Jason, Sheriff Welko's boy. The sheriff's kid."

"Yes, I know. I know who Jason is. I called him last minute to come babysit because you forgot. Remember?" Anita focused her attention on Craig.

"The sheriff's kid," Craig repeated.

"Is there something wrong?"

He pointed to the door with his eyes.

"Let's go. We should check on the girls," he whispered.

"The girls are fine." Anita pointed to the chairs. "I think we should stay. I think they're going to play some kind of party game."

"Oh, do you have go?" Mela said, looking at Craig. "Honey, I was hoping you'd stay and play with us."

"You see. It's Duck, Duck, Goose or something." Anita frowned.

"Mela, we can't stay. Anita, let's go, now." Craig's voice was firm and hurried.

Anita didn't like his tone now or earlier when it was filled with accusation. "I think we should stay and play."

"Oh, oh, the Goodwins are having an argument." David reached up from his chair to hold Anita's hand. "Let Anita stay if she wants to. We'll take care of her. You don't need to worry. You can go check on those beautiful girls of yours and we can take her home."

"Yes, I've been with the girls all day." Anita gripped his hand tight. "Why don't *you* look after them for a while?"

"Anita, come on. You're drunk," Craig said.

"I am not drunk." Anita released David's hand and took a gulp from her plastic cup.

"You're being ridiculous."

"Am I?" She took another swallow.

"Yes." He stared right into her eyes. "This isn't the time."

She pulled up her neckline. "I'm staying. I won't leave. I'm in it for the long haul."

"What are you talking about?" He lifted his hands in the air.

She waved her hand with the drink toward the room and clear liquid splashed to floor. She was going to fit in here come hell or high water, she thought. Pleased that her in-laws' saying came so quickly to mind, she sat.

"Anita, I'm sorry about what I said earlier." Craig put his hands in prayer position.

"In it for the long haul," Anita said.

"I *will* leave you here." Craig's eyes glowed green like a prickly yucca.

"Good-bye." She stared right back.

"Well then, you should get those private school girls of yours to bed," Mela said. "I do love vanilla."

"Where are my damn keys?" Craig said.

"They're in the bucket where you dropped them," Anita said. "It's for sober drivers only."

"Craig, you don't have to go. Let me call your sitter. It's Jason, right?" Jim fumbled in his pocket for his cell phone. "He's Sheriff Welko's oldest. We're all great friends. They go skiing with us all the time. He was in Aspen with us this last trip. He's a great kid. He can handle anything that comes his way. He's handled plenty, believe you me."

Craig combed through the bucket frantically. He dug out a Texas A&M key chain with ten keys attached.

"He picked me. He picked me." Mela laughed. "Now, you *have* to stay. It'll be a soft swap."

"No, I have to get home," Craig said. "Anita, we should get home, now."

Anita felt uneasy and confused but mostly angry. Mela's words sounded oddly sexual. Craig had accused her too many times of not being sexual. How could he expect her to be sexual after a full day with three little girls? Hours of mindless tea and princess parties, endless arguments, and high-pitched squealing. His long nights at the shop and his obsession with customers made her feel invisible. When he did notice her, it was for one thing only. At those times he was no better than Jim. She turned her back to Craig and talked to David.

"Thanks, you all. I had a really good time," Craig said as the door slammed shut.

"It was my keys he picked out of the bucket. I was picked," Jim said as he sat next to Anita.

Acknowledgments

I dedicated this book to my father, Jose Andres Granados, as a thank-you. He died December 14, 2014. He was the abanderado of the Granados family. His stories sustained and nourished me, and I miss them.

To the men in my immediate family, Ken Esten, Esten Andres, and William Celestino Cooke, I say thanks. Your existence in this world fills me with so much pride and joy that my cup runneth over, in much the same way the clothes hamper in your rooms do. I'd like to thank Corina Granados, Rebecca Granados, Jose Andres Granados, Abel Granados, my Califas family, my El Paso family, and my Rockdale family for their love and tolerance; Sheryl Luna, Diana Lopez, Joel Salcido, and Dagoberto Gilb for their continuing friendship and support; Lowell Mick White, Carmen Edington, and David Duhr for their help with the manuscript; and Harold Parsley and the Book Mates Reading Club in Rockdale for their love of literature and optimism about the written word. Books and book clubs make life better. Last but not least, I'd like to thank the University of New Mexico Press not only for publishing these stories but for existing. Through their efforts on these pages and with their booklist, Elise McHugh and the entire staff at UNM Press are helping give a voice to working-class Mexican American lives, which are often overlooked by mainstream publishers. Son bravos.